A ndrew Murray Scott was born in Aberdeen and is now based at Broughty Ferry where he lives with his wife Frances.

He graduated in English and Modern History and his first novel, *Tumulus*, won the inaugural Dundee Book Prize in 1999, being described as 'a *tour de force*, the work of an extremely talented, confident, sophisticated and imaginative writer'. He has written two further novels, *Estuary Blue* and *The Mushroom Club*, as well as a number of nonfiction books.

To Ann,
With Best wishes,

The Big J

ANDREW MURRAY SCOTT

Steve Savage
LONDON AND EDINBURGH

Steve Savage Publishers Ltd
The Old Truman Brewery
91 Brick Lane
LONDON
E1 6QL

www.savagepublishers.com

Published in Great Britain by Steve Savage Publishers Ltd 2008

ISBN 978-1-904246-33-6

Typeset by Steve Savage Publishers Ltd
Printed and bound by The Cromwell Press Ltd

Here comes the piteous prince
His young flesh torn, his fair head bruised

Euripides, *Hippolytus*

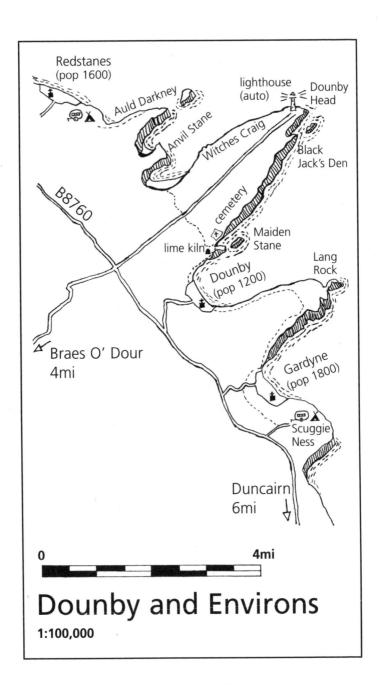

Redstanes
(pop 1600)

Auld Darkney

lighthouse
(auto)

Dounby
Head

Anvil Stane

Witches Craig

Black
Jack's Den

B8760

cemetery

Maiden
Stane

lime kiln

Lang
Rock

Dounby
(pop 1200)

Braes O' Dour
4mi

Gardyne
(pop 1800)

Scuggie
Ness

Duncairn
6mi

0   4mi

Dounby and Environs

1:100,000

I

Big J still lives there, gazing out on that salty horizon like a lifer through his bars. It's a pure tragedy. And everywhere you look there's gulls jeering and gyring slowly in an updraught. They're always mocking us: they couldn't care less: we're just something they try to shit on. Way down below, red roofs, whitewashed walls and narrow streets unwind slowly to the ancient harbour. This is Dounby, a grimy smudge on the rim of the North Sea whose waters undercut it with every tide. The name of the place half rhymes the sound of the waves booming under cliffs, a sort of chorus in two parts for the ocean and the land. Not much of a name either – two syllables – to label a post office, a wooden gospel hall, a tiny, one-roomed branch of the Bank of Scotland and a dozen or so little shops. There are two hotels: the Norseman Inn and the Dounby Hotel, with public bars. There's a concrete-box public toilet with corrugated iron roof, which opens during the summer months. Padlocked and shuttered during the winter because no one comes here then. There's a seasonal tearoom that caters for the air-conditioned mega-coaches that bump and jolt carefully down the steep narrow road to the tarmacked car park halfway down the cliff from the end of April to September. We used to laugh at the white faces of the coach drivers – and smell the burning brakes.

The view from the car park is familiar to folks the world over from calendars and tourist brochures with captions such as: *The quaint fishing harbour of Dounby is a must-see daytrip when visiting the city of Duncairn.* You're bound to have heard of Dounby. Lots of folk come to visit, but not many would like it if they had to live here all year round. Visitors stay for twenty minutes on average (we've timed them). A couple of snaps, quick stroll on the pier, a cup of tea, then gone. But we have to stay here forever. Even when we've left we never really get away. I don't come back often now that my mother and stepfather have moved away.

Everyone that hears about Dounby says how beautiful it is. Well, it's bare and huge, a soaring empty sky that makes you feel pretty small and insignificant. There's something amazing about the light – almost as powerful as X-rays – and the impressive sandstone stacks, worked red raw by salty winds and grasping tides into funny apple-core shapes. I can see it or think about it like a tourist would. And then, a funny thing happens... Standing at the bend up on the main road, by the black-lettered roadsign that spells *Dounby*, I suddenly feel a catch in my throat because it's like looking down on my past. I get the feeling that leaving the place was a kind of betrayal. And the funny thing is – it's a person I'm thinking about. Not my grandfather nor any of my great-uncles who fought in the war – an incomer: someone I only met in the few months before I left for University. The Big J. The J bit rhymes with 'guy' by the way; that's the way we pronounce it up here. He seems, in a funny kind of way, to represent the place for me, which makes the betrayal all the worse. I betrayed him and the place. Big J. He must've had a real name but we never found out what it was and anyway we preferred nicknames. Our full names seemed too pompous and formal for such a tucked-away wee place of twelve hundred lost souls perched on the rim of the sea.

Anyway, he was a couple of years older than we were. In that final summer, Alan Muir and I were seventeen but J was already an adult. He sort of became our sun god, the one we gossiped about, tried to win praise off of. For years afterwards, I imitated the way he was, his cool manner. He was ultra-cool, a long tall cool dude. In my imagination, he somehow dominates that long endless boring year of waiting to be told I was an adult. And of course the tragedy – that changed everything. So, coming back to the place, I think of Big J, even if I don't see him and I remember what happened to him. And then I immediately think of someone else, with a name as improbable in Dounby as you could possibly imagine: Xanthe Pritchard-Benz. From Boston, Massachusetts, USA. You could say she caused all the trouble, but that's not really fair. Not her fault she was so gorgeous.

I first met her when I got the paper-round from Mr McGovern at the Spar. I couldn't believe my luck at the time, then I found no one else wanted the job. Most of the deliveries were up in the bungalows and you got two measly pence for each paper you delivered. Xanthe, or Mrs Pritchard as she was known, lived in that ugly new house at the very top of the hill whose plate glass windows overlook the bay. She often came to the door in a kimono-type robe. I thought she was right glamorous. In the winter, the house was locked up and she was away to America. Dounby was just her holiday place. After I gave up the paper-round when I was thirteen, I became a sort of odd-job boy for her, cutting the grass – there was loads of it on all sides of the house – and weeding and getting messages for her and that kind of thing. I admit I had fantasies about her. That maybe she'd turn out to be my secret aunt or a cousin and take me away to America with her. But that all ended when she arrived one year with a man called Oliver. I hated him on sight. They arrived in early May.

I had waited for a whole day to give her time to unpack and after breakfast next morning stuffed my wellies into a plastic bag in case I would get weeding to do.

'I'll be back for tea,' I told my mother at the back door.

My stepfather looked up from his huge black bible. Glanced at the wellington boots. 'The Sabbath day means nothing to you?' he muttered. 'Thou shalt do no labour...'

My mother clicked her tongue in reproval. 'Robbie's only helping out where he's needed.'

The road was black and slippery. Under the lee of the cliffs there was coldness in the air. At the top of the Braeheid, I looked back at the sweep of the bay, flat calm and featureless just like always. Then I turned into their drive at the top of the hill and saw a new vehicle, a black 4x4 Range Rover. It was a top of the range model, almost brand new. I was examining it when I heard a man's shout from the house.

'Oi you! Chummy! What d'you want here?' He came towards me, a bullish man, powerfully built, wearing corduroys, checked shirt and tie with a green padded shooting vest. His heavy face was perspiring and red and what remained of his hair was glossy black. He stood between the door and me, aiming the lit end of a cigar in my direction, and then shouted over his shoulder. 'Hey, babe, we have a visitor!'

Mrs Pritchard emerged smiling from the front door. 'Robert! Lovely to see you!' It seemed at that moment that her greeting was rather false, but I was prepared to accept that I might be being over-sensitive. I did not expect her to hug me and kiss me on the cheek however – there in front of that man.

'Robert, this is Oliver, my man-friend,' she said smoothly. 'He'll be staying with us this summer and this is—'

I gaped like a dumbo at the girl who stood in the doorway.

'—Tara, Oliver's niece.'

When I turned back to Mrs Pritchard, she was smiling archly. 'I see that I've lost an admirer,' she said and gave me a dirty big wink.

'I've come to see if you need me for anything,' I said, blushing. I tried to ignore the terrible innuendo of the words which I was sure would drive the man into a frenzy but no one seemed to have noticed. Oliver just grunted and slouched off into the house.

Mrs Pritchard took my arm and led me around the front garden. 'It's very kind of you, Robert. I didn't expect it. The place has gone to rack and ruin since we've been away. I'd very grateful if you could help.' Her words, and her closeness, conspired to give me shivers up my spine and a strange warmth that I found embarrassing. I felt at that moment that I would have done anything for Xanthe Pritchard-Benz, except look her in the eye. She was, at that time, I suppose, pretty old, in her mid-thirties maybe, but the years sat easily on her. She was well toned, slightly muscular and darkly tanned. I suspected that some private dentist in America had fixed her teeth. They were too perfect, too white somehow. She was always smiling. Smiling as she pushed back her long dark hair and something about the way she smiled and tossed her head never failed to entice me. It was rare for her legs and arms to be entirely covered. Sometimes she wore backless dresses that made it easy to count the vertebrae of her spine as they slid into the cleft of her bottom. Such alien style black affronted Dounby which was tight-knit and religious. I was so aware then of the thin layer of cotton between her body and mine and looked out at the sea in case she could read the thoughts showing on my face.

I listened to her in a half-daze as she talked about the grass and the weeds and the plans she and Oliver were making for the summer. They were going to buy a boat. Oliver had business ideas and she planned to do so *many* artworks. She planned to tidy the shed and lay on electricity and use it as a forge for her sculptures. I liked the way she talked to me as if I was an old pal, just the sound of her voice giving me goosebumps.

'I've so many ideas, Robert. So much work to do. I must find a local blacksmith who could lend me some equipment. Do you know of someone?'

Oliver appeared on the veranda at the front of the house with a large drink in his hand. 'Babe, put that boy down,' he instructed. 'You don't know where he's been.' He peered at me from under his heavy eyebrows. 'He's a little too mature for my liking. I hope he's not a new toyboy?' He laughed and I didn't like it at all.

Mrs Pritchard smoothed my hair at the front. 'He's lovely, my Robert,' she purred. 'If I ever do take a toyboy, he'll be first in line.' To me, she said, as we moved out of earshot: 'What do you think of Oliver, dear, isn't he a whole lot of man?'

'Well…' I mumbled.

She laughed at my embarrassment. 'There's a lot more to him than meets the eye. Oh, there I go again! You don't like him, I guess.'

'Well…'

'Now, don't be jealous, Robert. We'll still be friends.' She put her arm around me and steered me between two overgrown rhododendrons. Just for a second I thought she was going to kiss me again. Her face was close to mine.

'Tell me, Robert,' she said softly, 'you know everyone around here. The locals I mean. Who is that boy with the motorcycle and... um... sideburns... good-looking...'

I knew instantly whom she meant. She seemed amused at his name.

'Hmn,' she murmured. 'Is he a special friend of yours?'

'I don't really know him,' I said. 'No one does. He's an incomer.'

'And so am I,' she laughed triumphantly. 'So we've that in common.'

* * *

But even I was an incomer. My family roots lay further inland among the generations of hinds and quinies – farm servants – from the cotter villages of Auchtergat, Auldloof and Braes O' Dour. Cemeteries there are populated with grandfathers and uncles and great-uncles of mine. In Montquhitter Parish Churchyard at Cuminestown my father's name – the same as mine – chiselled in the sparkling stone, never fails to give me a jolt. Our surname, Strachan, common around here, is pronounced locally 'Stron' and there's loads of them around. Facing my father's stone, across neatly cut, well-watered grass, is the headstone of my great uncle Dod and Lizzie his wife, who had the farm, thirty acres, on the hill at South Thornhill, where my father played as a boy. But he died when I was ten, and two years later, my mother married again. We moved to the coast, eight miles away, and I became part of that close-knit tribe of a dozen who grew up amongst the jeering applause of seagulls.

And the seagulls, or their descendants, are hovering yet, like the familiars of the dead generations. Looking over the dyke now, ten years later, I observe the light shift dramatically along the coast. Strong beams burst the clouds and torch the leaden water a mile offshore. We used to gaze on that oblivious, endless, featureless horizon. We didn't love it as we could love a tree, or a beach or the sheltered lee of a hill, or something from nature: we feared it. It didn't interest us. It was a blank mirror and we stared into it hoping to see brighter prospects. And still staring into it is Big J – strangely diminished – for he remained in Dounby. And that's the saddest thing of all. I don't know him now, of course, I mean I don't talk to him, but I still think of him a lot. I am a pale imitation of him; find myself acting, in certain circumstances, like he would act. He made such an impression on the seventeen-year-old me.

I first heard of him the year before. We were sitting in the ramshackle boatshed by the Coble Landing, a hundred yards across shingle from the harbour wall. It was a dark, filthy interior, rank with woodsmoke, battered by the surly voices of the sea.

'We've got new neighbours, Robbie,' Lila Matheson told me in a crackling, fizzing interlude. Breaking a stick into bits between her fists, her fingers protruded raw from black woollen gloves. 'Looks like a boy and his aunt – or maybe his mother, but she seems dead old, somehow.' The surge broke around us, salt spray rattling the corrugated iron walls, dissolving the mortar walls of the old jetty. Tossing the sticks into the fire we had made in a rusted oil drum, she muffled her palms together. 'Probably an alkie. Yvie says they're like a pair of tinks.'

I could see part of her face in the orange glow. We were muffled up in thick jerseys, coats, balaclavas and wellies. I pondered what she had said as the spray exploded into shrapnel. It was unlike Yvie to be so casually dismissive. The flames shifted the sticks, threw faster shadows. It was early February. The storm was riding on high winds and the low rumble of seething waters unsettled the shingle. Damp wood sputtered in the fire. But there was no heat somehow in those flames. Shared by the half-dozen of us, it was too sparse to go round.

'Wonder if he'll be on the bus on Monday?' Alan said after a few contemplative moments. He rubbed his nose vigorously with a crumpled cloth.

'Likely, if he's ages with us.' Rob Lowdy clattered the side of the brazier with his steel toe-capped boot. A few sparks burst in the air and sifted back into the flames. 'They'll send the boy to the Academy. Another brick in the wall.'

But they didn't and the new boy wasn't heard of for several weeks. We had troubles of our own: with exams coming up and having to stay in to study. The parents practically demanded it. We still found time to head down to the Beach Café most evenings. I'd call for Alan who lived across the street at number 24. Hands in pockets, we'd sidle down the road, take a shortcut off down narrow concrete steps, through tiny back gardens and by whitewashed gable walls to emerge at the harbour. The big wooden shed leaned against the upper harbour wall. It had two doors, one for the café and the other for the arcade but there was only one room, separated by a stack of cardboard crates and a cream-coloured deep-freeze where Sandy Stokes stored engine parts – to the dismay of the occasional tourist who lifted the lid expecting ice-cream.

Sandy was leaning against the counter boring the twins, Yvie and Lila Matheson, about San Francisco and all the times he'd had in London in the 60s. Personally, I didn't think Sandy had been as far as Redstanes or Gardyne, let alone the metropolis, but in a small place like Dounby you'd to show restraint – I didn't want to get barred. There was nowhere else indoors to meet, unless you count the hall of the Church of The Second Chance – and you'd only go there if you were desperate or out of your tree – or the Adventists' cemetery up on the hill. There's a crypt there you can sit in, but it only seats three and even then you get the wind in your face.

'... a spin when I get the "li'l deuce coupe" fixed up...' I heard him saying as I came in. 'Just got to weld on some new gaskets then it'll be all systems go.' He caressed the long grey hair behind his ear.

'Then beam me up, Scotty,' Yvie muttered, drawing on her rolly-up.

I put coins in the drinks machine, selected Irn Bru and it clunked out the bottom. I joined Alan and the girls at the window table that looks out onto the dark, fungused stones of the harbour wall.

Sandy stood at the counter, thumbs hooked around the belt loops of his baggy denims, striplight gleaming on his bald patch. 'What can I do you for?' he'd grin, scratching his belly. It was his catchphrase. He asked everyone, male and female: 'What'll it be, darlin? Just ask – and I'll give you one!' He stood there season after season waiting for someone to place an order from the handwritten, fly-spattered menu card tacked to the wall behind him. No one ever did. There had been a rumour that he did not have the equipment or the supplies to provide any of the items on it anyway. No one who came into the Beach Café ordered anything other than a slice of cake or a scone to go with a cup of tea or something from the drinks machine. If some big spender had come strolling in and ordered the Spanish omelette, odds on Sandy would have fainted clear away. According to my stepfather, who was a stickler for rules of all kinds, he did not have a hot food licence. As for the coupe, that was something of a seven-day wonder, an actual American classic car – or automobile, as Sandy preferred to call it – here in Dounby. But not a '32 Ford, in case that's what you thought: a Lincoln Continental. It was in the garage, axles up on blocks, while Sandy attempted to sort out exactly what was wrong with its whitewall tyres, or fiddled with something else that had gone wrong with it. Sometimes he just sat in the car with his shades on, pretending he was tearing up Highway 1. We'd watched him through a hole in the wall. We felt dead sorry for him but that didn't stop us urinating into the petrol tank now and then just for a laugh.

'That new lad that moved in across the way from us,' said Lila, sharing her ciggie with me, 'mind, I told yous a few weeks ago?' She looked around for confirmation. 'Well, seems he's already left school. Think he's signing on. The old woman is his aunt, well, she's no his mother. Too old.'

'What guy is this?' Alan was quick to ask. He'd been going out with Lila ever since I could remember and didn't like her talking about an incomer with such obvious interest.

'Says his name is Big J.' Lila sniffed. 'Calls the woman Auntie Ellen, but I get the impression they're no blood relatives.'

'Big J? What kind of doss name is that?' Alan wanted to know. 'Where's he from?'

Lila shrugged. 'Glasgow, I think. Or Paisley? Some city place.'

'And you've been chatting him up?'

Heather came in. 'Talking about the tinky family?' she asked. 'The J-guy?' Rob was behind her. Eyebrows were raised at that, particularly by Yvie, I noticed. Not many blokes were best pals with their own wee sisters. Rob's the best-looking guy around according to the girls. They once took a vote on it. Personally, I think his ears are too big. I'd always liked Heather though she was three years younger than me, which is bordering on child-molestation. She was nearly the same height as me all the same.

'He's a huu-nnnk, him!' Heather moaned. 'Tall boy, right? Slim and that? Wears his shades all the time. I chatted to him a wee bit in the Shoprite. He's bloody gorgeous!'

We chewed it over later as we drifted down to the harbour wall. 'Big J?' Alan pronounced sourly. 'A Weegie from the slums. What's he here for, anyway?' He got up on the dyke and scanned the empty horizon.

'To rape and pillage maybe?' I suggested, lobbing a stone at an evil-looking gull that was hanging around. 'Maybe he's heard about the great nightlife in Dounby? Our nightclubs, discos, the theme bars...'

That earned me a sour look. 'More likely been released from some jail. Care in the community maybe.'

'Give him a chance,' Yvie said, sitting down on a stack of McAdam's plastic fishboxes. 'He might be dead nice and that. We could do with new faces round here.' She began to comb her beaded braids with her funny wooden comb. Yvie tried to be 'soul sister' number one, but she's not as pretty as Lila. Lila's hair was long and jet black while Yvie's was now sort of blonde, sort of red and done up in tight braids that I hated the look of. To me, that style looked kind of dirty, like manky straw.

'City boys never fit in,' Alan grumbled. 'Not for long, anyway. He won't be staying around.'

'That's up to him. See you tomorrow.'

* * *

I seemed to see less of my pals once the school bus had deposited us at Duncairn Academy. We were all in different classes. Even Alan I only saw in subjects like RI and PE, during library periods and of course, the breaks. We got picked up at the bend by the filling station at the top of the hill. It was a scramble to get up there by twenty past eight. Often, the paths around the back gardens would be swallowed up by an early-morning haar. Dounby has its own. The oldies call it the sea-fret as if the sea's a person having moods. Sometimes the bus was late but it always appeared, never broke down, even though it was an ancient old dinosaur from the steam age. Anyway, the journey took half an hour, the Academy being on the south side of Duncairn. It was an almost new, low, breeze-block construction dating from the 1970s, whose harling was already coming off in patches, aided by the steel toe-capped boots of the small fry which us older guys referred to as 'snots' or 'sperms'. The school struggled under the iron regime of Von Blofeld the 'Heedie' – Mr Bloomfield – who shaved his skull everyday and covered it with a shiny sort of oil. The only hair on him was in his nostrils – and he had more in there than Mr Buckman had on the entire back of his head. He used to pull a sinister leer when patrolling the lavvy block, sniffing for reefers or used condoms. Just one crooked tooth showing at the side of his mouth. His voice scared pigeons off the roof and that was when he was just talking to you in the playground. He was Satan in a grey suit and Hush Puppies. In his office he had a real Lochgelly, two-pronged, black twisted leather – the real deal – framed in a long glass display case on the wall behind his chair. He probably took it out to sniff now and then because belting had been banned. Although I was taller than he was, I hid if I saw him coming.

Being in the fifth year, we had a room up at the top of the stairs in the Languages block. The girls had their own common room so ours was always rowdy with three-card brag schools, or mucking about, and some blokes swapped porny mags. In the summer you could get out onto the fire escape and sunbathe on the roof if you were an exhibitionist or not bothered that some seagulls'd shite on you or the others'd nick your things. Someone did that once and the poor bugger had to streak about the classrooms trying to find where his gear had been posed. The String Bean got wind of it and there was a lot of trouble. Someone got excluded for it. A lot of football got played on the tarmac, scuffling with a tennis ball in teams of twenty in front of goals chalked on the bike sheds, but that ended in my second last year, the year Duncairn won the European Cup against some team from Italy. I remember seeing the team on the top of an open-deck bus in the High Street, surrounded by the entire population of the place, a hundred and twenty thousand at least. They were like tubby dwarfs, the opposite of the tall, slim Italians. We got the day off school for that. It was a big deal for Duncairn. But when you got to S4, you had a certain dignity and scuffing about with hordes of snots and sperms was beneath you.

We didn't go to Duncairn much even when we were there if you know what I mean. Sometimes we'd meet up at lunchtime and go for a wander down to the docks and the ferry terminal, but mostly we hung about the common room or smoked at the back of the toilet block. We hardly ever went in the evenings. It was too far to bother. Mostly we just stayed around Dounby, mucking about.

Most folk who visit Dounby stand about at the harbour looking daft for a couple of minutes as if they've suddenly realised there's nowhere else to go. They click off a few snaps, jump back in the car and drive slowly up the hill, gawping left and right at the wee houses. They're all thinking the same thing. You can almost see their lips moving. But when you live here you know there's nothing quaint about it. It's really six separate communities stuck together: The oldest part is the houses around the Harbour that are mostly crumbling to bits. Then there's several rows of tiny damp houses facing each other on the flat bit known as the New Ground. On the other side of the harbour is the Seatown; terraces of a hundred or so whitewashed houses that stretch out to the beach. It used to be dead old and manky but some of the houses have been bought by outsiders and are rented out to holidaymakers. Artists and various posers of one sort or another, mostly English, whom you never really meet. You can tell their places by the netting and old lobster creels outside which have been tarted up as decoration. The houses are so close together that if somebody farts in bed all the people in the street can smell it. There are handrails built into the house walls so you can walk up and down the passageways when it's icy. Some of the houses at the far end are just shacks – with tin roofs. Breeks lived with his stepmother in one of those. Above the Seatown and the Harbour is the Braeheid that has a few terraces and lots of shops, some B & Bs and the two hotels. Above that is the Council Houses – where I live – and above that, climbing up over the cliffs, is the Bungalows: posh detached houses, some holiday homes and chalets. That's where Mrs Pritchard's house is, at the end, off by itself. And further along the cliff, one tosser who lives there, an old admiral or something, flies a huge Union Jack off a pole. That pisses everybody off – you can see the thing for miles – and Hecky often talks about burning it down. But anyway, I live in the council estate and Alan lives across the street.

Alan's father, Hecky, works on the *Summer Star*, an old rust-bucket with third-hand radar and the kind of equipment that only just scrapes through each year's inspection. Hecky seemed to take a perverse pleasure in that. It tied up at Gardyne. No big boats worked out of Dounby, no boats at all except a couple of crabbers and a charter boat for the line fishing and day trips. There were some pleasure craft, yachts and the like, tied up at the harbour and a lot more that were for sale or had been left to rust or were undergoing some pretence of repair. There was even the hulk of a thirty-four-foot trawler, *Lucky Dog*, sunk at her berth, which had been there as long as I can remember. You could see the fish going in and out of her on sunny days. But with new crises in fishing, Hecky considered himself lucky to get one trip a month though it might last up to two weeks and take them deep into Arctic waters, if it was one of those huge purse-seine netters. In the summer he signed on.

'Aye, aye, wi all the regulations and this and that the skipper's to contend wi, it's a wonder we get put to sea at all,' he'd say, sitting on the doorstep with a can of superlager for his breakfast. Then he'd roll a cigarette with the flat, square fingers of one hand and give out the familiar warning: 'Don't ever gang to the fishing, lads. Game for mugs.'

Neither Alan nor I had any thoughts about it. If we did live with our toes in the North Sea, our backs were to it and our futures firmly inland, south. Too much of the history of Dounby is about wrecks and drownings and the fickle two fingers of watery fate. The sea was our enemy, something to avoid. Alan had grown up with the lore and the rumours of black fish landings, dope smuggling and other entrepreneurial activities. Hecky was always full of it. Dope smuggling sounded to us like a better idea than fishing but the risks still weren't worth it, unless you were the Mr Big of the whole deal. And no self-respecting Mr Big would be caught anywhere near a boat or the sea. As for fishing, you'd be better paid as a toilet attendant.

'There's nothing like it, lads,' he'd tell us, wistfully, after a certain number of cans of the superlager. 'Aye, aye, when you're out, just you and the boat, the sea and your mates, like. Just letting the tide drive you in – and then you see the headland like a distant island.' He glared up to see if we were laughing at him – but we were like High Court judges. 'Lads,' he'd go, swigging his beer, 'lads, that's when you feel you're alive. No just living.'

Hecky was half-mad, even before he started at the drinking. Even Alan thought so and of course, Alan's mum had buggered off years ago, so she must have thought so too. Like, he wore an earring because he believed it would protect him from drowning and getting diseases and all sorts. 'It's a bit o fisher's magic, lads, aye.' He'd nod and spit. 'Aye, fisher folk have been wearin earrings since the fifteen hunders,' he'd say, trying to sound wise. We'd just laugh at him. 'Aye, and drownin since then, an all,' we'd say. He'd just guffaw and ignore us. Once he'd got to the sentimental stage we knew he was near to passing out and when he passed out, we'd help ourselves to any surplus cans and go down to the Coble Landing and leave him to sleep it off. Sometimes Hecky palled up with his mate, Billy Murrell and went out crabbing around the bay or line fishing around the coves. Alan had been out with them once or twice when he was younger.

'Quite liked it, Robbie, isn't that funny?' he said one night in his room. We were fed up of playing with the new Playstation, just lying there on his bed looking out at the rain on the skylight, listening for the thunder. 'We saw lots of seals, riving at the nets, the greedy buggers.' He grinned sadly. 'We just left them to it, ken. Though sometimes Bill takes a shotgun and has a go. Anyway, this time we got a salmon, decent size too. Hauled it in and knocked it over the head. That was the good bit. But we were out the whole day and it got right boring y'ken. I ended up sleeping in the bottom of the boat. Then it started pishin rain. Just like now. It's always bloody raining.'

I looked up from knotting the laces on my trainers. 'This Billy's boat you were on?'

He shook his head. 'Na. Wee boat my dad used to have. A twenty footer, open boat like. Leaked like a bloody sieve. Had to bale her every ten minutes or she'd go under.'

'That right? Wouldn't get me out in a boat like that.'

'Ach, you could have used it to drain your cabbage. But we were never more than a mile out.'

After a few moments I asked him what had happened to the boat.

He rubbed at the pluke on his jaw. 'Hecky sold it, didn't he. Got a hundred quid for her.'

'Hundred quid? That all?'

'Fifty more than I'd give him,' Alan said earnestly, pushing his dark fringe out of his eyes. 'So now she's moored on the jetty at Gardyne. Been there years. Nobody uses her. Just lies there and rots.'

Then I suddenly remembered. 'Mrs Pritchard's going to buy a boat. Maybe she'll take me out in it.'

Alan gave me a funny look. 'You said you just cut her grass. What would she take you out on her boat for, eh?'

2

I never much liked the city of Duncairn, neither the place
nor the people. It'd almost doubled in size since the oil
was found offshore. Used to be a couthy place where local
farmers came to sell their produce but the farmers worked
on the rigs now and their daughters danced butt-naked
in steel cages in the go-go dancing bars. There was a
hardness about the place and that was all to do with
money. The getting of it and the spending of it quick. I
was used to travelling the eleven miles by bus though,
rather than car.

'How old are you now, Bob?' Oliver asked, squinting
at me as he rolled up the sleeves on his hairy arm, steering
with his elbow. The Range Rover careered along the dual
carriageway. 'I guess about sixteen?'

'I'm seventeen,' I said, 'and nobody calls me Bob.'

'Time enough to get with the girlies,' he said nastily. 'Got
a special girl? Anyone who tickles your fancy so to speak?'

'No.'

'Go on. I bet you've had lots of practice.'

'I have not.'

He took the bend too fast and I found myself gripping
the cushion of the seat. We were already near the big
roundabout and the bridge over the River Cairn on the
outskirts of the city.

He peered at me and grinned. 'Enjoying the ride? A good set of wheels,' he said appraisingly. 'Handles well. You don't drive then, Bob?'

'Robbie,' I corrected. 'I'm getting driving lessons soon.'

'Man needs a set of wheels if he wants to get the birds. Get yourself a car, boy. Do the training, eh? Back-seat engineer. Learn where to fit the crankshaft, eh?' He began to brake for the roundabout. Rain glistened on the windscreen. I hated all his innuendo. I hated being near him. This trip to Duncairn was all his idea, right out of the blue. I'd been dreading it for days.

'Here we are: Duncairn,' he pronounced. 'Known for its tarts. We'll have to watch ourselves. The women here can count what's in your wallet before you even get it out.' He grinned sideways at me. 'If you know what I mean.'

New private housing estates sprawl on the north side of Duncairn and they are every bit as depressing as the older council housing schemes on the other side of the wide ring road. They seem peripheral and out of place, the kind of suburbia you expect in southern English cities, red-brick with mock-Tudor arches and tiny garden rectangles. Brick and concrete mazes with ironic pleasant-sounding names. Then we were stuck in heavy traffic of buses and overloaded lorries, waiting for traffic lights to change.

'So what's your poison?' Oliver asked as he waited at a junction in the lane marked for the city centre. 'Let me guess – you're a lager kind of chap?'

'Yeah, that's all right,' I admitted grudgingly. 'That's usually what I drink.'

'Thought so.' He seemed pleased. 'We'll have a good day out, trust your uncle Oliver.'

I glanced at the expensive watch clamped around his hairy wrist and shuddered. I didn't like the idea of being related to him even as a joke. Also, I remembered my uncles and the kind of men they had been. Oliver was a different sort, all shifty and slimy and easy charm. It didn't help that he was a southerner. People from those parts seemed to have an inbuilt shiftiness, a lack of probity. There was something of the Arthur Daley about him.

'Trust your uncle Oliver,' he repeated several times, concentrating on driving in the increasingly narrow streets. 'We'll have fun. Oho, me boyo,' he exulted. 'There's a space.'

He found what was probably the only empty parking space in the entire city centre and expertly inserted the 4x4 into it. 'Out you get,' he instructed.

He inserted a stream of coins into the meter and stuck the ticket inside the windscreen.

'Right, Bob, Duncairn awaits!'

We were at the lower end of a street that runs from the main shopping area down to the harbour. I had been there many times in my lunch hour, by myself or with others in my class. But I was seeing it through different eyes somehow, since now I was not dressed as a schoolboy. I followed him down the pavement in the slight smirring rain, hands in the pockets of my leather jerkin. Ahead of us were the funnels and masts of the ships in port.

He turned at the bottom of the street. 'Come on,' he said. 'Along here.' He led me into Harbour Lane, a constricted street that runs along the dockside. I scurried to catch up with him. 'Anyone asks,' he said, 'you're eighteen. All right?'

'Course.'

I followed him through the narrow doorway into the Mandrake Bar. It was crowded with noisy, rough boozers, most of whom seemed bigger than me. I felt sure they'd all know I was underage so I didn't look at anyone in case they sussed me out. Oliver pushed through the tobacco smoke curtain to the bar.

'Lager and a double Bells,' he ordered loudly.

I knew by intuition the sort of place it was. There were women of a particular kind, hard-eyed, the sort who wore bright dresses under anoraks with trainers, whose make-up was a shade too thick, whose fingernails were painted but whose clothes reeked of sweat. And the men were nondescript. The longer you looked at them the less you saw.

'Hello, lovey,' a girl asked, looking down at me. 'Looking for business?'

'He's with me,' Oliver said brusquely handing me a pint. He looked her up and down. 'He doesn't go with cheap floozies.' The woman made no protest and seemed to dissolve into the crowd. 'U-uugh!' Oliver shuddered. 'What a trollop. Look at her. What'd she say to you?'

I shrugged. 'Nothing. Just asked if I was looking for business. I suppose she must be a prostitute?'

Oliver snorted. 'I'll say. Fifty if she's a day. Been on the game forty years I'd be willing to bet.'

The day had become even more unpleasant for a number of reasons. I hated Oliver's loudness, his southern arrogance. I just hated people seeing us together. I decided that if there was any trouble I was going to get out and make my own way home on the bus.

'Look at that one!' Oliver sneered. 'With the big bazookas. I wouldn't touch her with yours. Ready for another?'

While he was at the bar, I went to the toilet. It was round the back of the place and you had to step down onto a stone floor which was six inches lower than the bar floor, then squeeze past two fridge freezers that had been left in the corridor with their electric cables wound round them. The first toilet door had the crudely daubed sign 'Gents' painted on the glass above the doorhandle. I didn't look to see what was painted on the second door. There was a stone urinal, upon which in the dim light, I could see a fluorescent fungus sprouting from a single cistern tank above a narrow frosted glass panel. The cubicle door had no lock. I stood by the toilet bowl, which had no seat, and peed, holding the door closed with my left hand. There was an inch of liquid on the floor and the walls were covered in nasty graffiti. My eye fell on the misspelling in the line: 'Beware! Crabs in hear can limbo dance!'

As I was coming out of the gents, the woman who had spoken to me earlier was coming out of the bar.

'See your dad,' she hissed. 'That man's a bastard!'

When I got back to the part of the bar where we'd been standing, I could see him talking to a group of younger people. I wondered if he was chatting up the girl with them. She looked Scandinavian, quite pretty. She glanced briefly at me and smiled. Then Oliver was coming back.

'We'd better get out of here,' I told him. 'That woman you spoke to earlier... she might make trouble.'

He seemed amused. 'Fat chance. But we're going anyway, soon as you get that down you.' He raised his voice: 'This place gives me the creeps.'

I was relieved to be outside. The air was fresh with a hint of salt, the typical harbour smells. Seagulls wheeled over the dock wall, reminding me of the harbour at Dounby. I looked at my watch and wondered what the gang would be doing now. It was 2pm. My eyes felt that dazed way you get when you've drunk alcohol and come out into the bright light. Sort of knocks you giddy a bit, makes everything colourful.

'There's someone I think you should meet,' Oliver said. 'I'll rephrase that. Someone it'd do you good to meet.'

'Yeah?'

As we got back into the car, I was just relieved to be on the move. Somehow being with him in the car wasn't as bad as being with him in public. I had decided that I would never again get trapped into going anywhere with him. We had to stop at numerous traffic lights before he hit the wide double carriageway that runs along by the Esplanade sands to the golf courses near the mouth of the River Cairn. If we only got the sunshine – I always think when I'm in that area – the tourists would flock here. There's about three miles of beautiful clean sand any Spanish resort would die for. Oliver turned left, we crossed the wide bridge by the Cairnview pub and turned into an area of tiny old houses that line the river bank among some nice trees.

'This is the oldest part of the city,' I told him for no particular reason.

He grunted and looked round at me with amazement. 'Enough with your history. It's a little action you're needing, m'boy.'

He parked in front of a twee-looking semi-detached bungalow that had tiny leaded windows in its door panels and a honeysuckle tied to a trellis around its yellow door. A carved stone on the lintel above the door bore the date 1789 divided by a thistle motif into 17 and 89.

'Here we are boyo,' Oliver said briskly. 'Let your education begin! Come on then, out!'

He lifted the solid black knocker and rapped on the small door. Almost immediately a petite woman opened it. She was quite blonde – natural I thought – and looked bemusedly at him and then me. Oliver moved her backwards into the doorway and followed her. I thought at the time it was rather rude – as if he didn't want to be seen going inside, even though there was no one in the street – unless there was someone I couldn't see lurking in the trees.

'Come on, Bob!' he hissed from inside. 'And close the door.'

I found myself in a narrow hall. I could see that the rooms were small. Oliver pointed at me and told the woman my name. 'Friend of mine,' he said casually. 'A four-star virgin.'

I felt myself blush bright red when the woman looked at me.

'This is Tish,' Oliver said.

She was maybe older than I'd first thought. Her hair was done up in neat plaits tied with a pink ribbon. She was wearing blue and white striped dungarees and underneath, a white tee-shirt.

'I thought it's about time he did the business,' Oliver was saying. 'On me, of course.'

'I don't know what he's talking about,' I said, blushing.

Tish looked from him to me and smiled with a little less than full hilarity. 'If he wishes to...' she said.

'Eh? Course he does. You'll give him the full works, eh?'

I stood there dumfounded.

'Is this your dad?' she asked, nodding at Oliver.

'God no!' I exclaimed. Oliver laughed abruptly.

Tish gave me a funny look and left us. Oliver plucked my arm and led me into the living room. He tossed his jacket onto the sofa.

'Right then, Bob. Get in there and give her one!'

He must have seen the look on my face because he stepped back. 'What?' He peered at me. 'Not fancy her? Once she gets her kit off you'll be all right. I'm doing you a favour. No? Even if I'm paying. No? Sure? She's a lovely piece – and clean too,' he added hastily. He studied me.

'Still no? Well it's down to me is it? I'm not letting it go to waste. Stand aside young man.' He turned at the door. 'I'm surprised. I thought you'd be up for it. As the actress said to the bishop. Wait here. Won't be long. Sorry, no pun intended.'

I was trembling as I sat in the sofa and picked up the newspaper. I couldn't read it. I stood up. I tried to roll up a cigarette but my fingers wouldn't let me. I saw a packet on the mantelpiece so I took one and lit it. I didn't think she'd mind. There was no sound from the hall. He'd be in there with her. I shuddered at the thought of it. And the anger I felt about him and Xanthe. Maybe I would tell her about Tish. Then of course, I realised she probably wouldn't believe me. I'd be accused of making it up. She was bound to take his side. What a minger though! He was horrible. My hand was shaking as I flicked ash at the ashtray; some went onto the carpet. I scuffed it with my shoe. I wondered if I should scarper, maybe leave him a note. I looked around the room. A nice cosy place. Tish seemed nice. It was a shame she was a prostitute. There were family photographs on the mantelpiece. A wedding picture. She was – or had been – married to a blond-haired man in uniform. Maybe a fireman. I was relieved to see there were no pictures of kids. Then I started to fancy I heard noises. I didn't want to hear anything. Frankly, I didn't even want to be there. I sat down. After a moment or two I put on the TV. Horse-racing. I put the sound off but kept staring at the pictures. Then I heard them coming back. I scrambled to get the TV off.

Oliver came into the room buckling his belt. His shirt was undone, revealing the dark jungle on his chest and throat. 'Changed your mind, no?' he asked. He seemed out of breath. 'Give me a cigarette.'

I took another cigarette out of the packet and lit it for him. He sat on the sofa. He seemed tired, quieter.

'I need to go to the toilet,' I said.

'Okay,' he pointed over his shoulder. 'Hurry up, then we'll go.'

But I went into the wrong room. Tish was on all fours. It seemed to me as if she was trying to get up, hair straggling over her face. She gave me a wild and unfriendly look – I noticed the ten-pound notes on the carpet – before I got the door closed.

When I got back to the living room, Oliver was dressed, buttoning his jacket. 'Okay, squire,' he said, pushing me out into the hall. 'We're off.'

As we clambered into the car, I had to ask: 'Is she all right? I mean…?'

'Oh, yeah,' he said casually. 'She likes it rough. Rougher the better.'

'What about Xanthe – Mrs Pritchard?'

He laughed though there was no humour in it; it was definitely unpleasant. 'You wouldn't be thinking of telling her, would you, chummy? I wouldn't. Xanthe can take care of herself. Change the subject, eh? It's time to eat. Any idea where we can get a good nosh-up?'

'No,' I said. I found that I had a renewed bout of the shakes. I guessed it was because he had made me into a conspirator. I didn't know what he had done to Tish but I didn't like the idea of it.

'You must do. I mean, you've a lot better knowledge of this place than I have, chummy. How about pizza?'

The worst thing was that at that moment I realised that I was hungry. 'There's a place in Queen Street,' I said reluctantly. 'I sometimes go there.'

'Excell-ent! You'll have to direct me.'

The heat and music of the restaurant began to relax me. I had a double order of garlic bread – since he was paying – and a bottle of lager. I started to think about

Tish, trying to remember what she had looked like. The picture in my mind's eye remained vague; I couldn't picture her breasts or her face. All I could visualise was the clothes she had been wearing – and that wild look.

'So what did you do to her – Tish?'

He laughed. 'A gentleman never tells.'

'Is she... married? I saw photographs of her with a man. What does he think of it?'

He glanced at me with surprise. 'If he knows anything, he's a fool. I haven't known Tish long anyway. She's nice isn't she?' He peered at me.

'I suppose so.'

'You should have gone with her, you know. What are you saving yourself for? You won't get the chance again.'

I was on the verge of asking him what he meant by that, but the pizza arrived and I never got around to it.

3

A few days later, a crowd of us were kicking about at the Braeheid outside the Shoprite. We were dead bored and none of us had any money. We had about three fags between the lot of us.

'Comin to the séance?' Yvie asked me. She simpered in that annoying put-on way and added: 'Heather Lowdy will be there.'

'I asked that Big J too,' Lila said coolly.

Alan thrust his hands in the pockets of his fleece and glared at her. 'Who says there's a séance? I've not heard anything.'

'Well, there is,' Lila sniffed. 'Saturday. At the old limekiln, after dark. You don't have to come.'

'Oh, I'll come all right. You're going, Robbie?'

'Aye. What else is there to do round here?'

'And Heather'll be there,' Yvie cooed, patting my wrist.

'You're real funny!'

'What is it with you and Heather?' Catto sneered. 'You getting married or what?' It was like Raymond Catto to go over the score. If he'd had a brain, he'd have been dangerous.

'Up yours, Catto-pus!'

'Look at his minter!'

'*Min-ter*!'

It's true I do blush easily sometimes. The more I protested the more they jeered. 'Just because I talked to her once,' I shouted. 'Just because I went to the flicks in Gardyne with Rob and she came along... she's only fourteen!' I was getting fed up with all the innuendo. Truth was, I did like Heather and she was grown up for her age but there was no way. We were just mates. Three years' age difference is a huge gulf when you're teenagers. Even in a small place like Dounby, where incest and sex with sheep is rife, if you listen to the rumours. And of course, I was keen on oily Oliver's niece Tara, whom I'd barely spoken to.

'Where you goin on your honeymoon, lover?' Lila asked.

'Robbie-Strachan-loves-Heather-Lowdy,' Yvie mocked in a singsong voice.

'Gie's a break!'

'True or false?'

I stood up and lobbed my Carlie can in the bin from twenty feet. *Impressive!* Even swotting for the Physics Higher had to be better than this.

'Awa to see Hot-arse Lowdy?' one snot-nosed sperm piped up from the telephone box once I was safely out of kicking range.

'Aye no doubt,' one of the small fry replied. 'These fourteen-year-olds are ace at the blow-jobs, I heard!'

'Awa for a quickie...'

'Ach grow up, ye wee tubes!'

'Robbie!' Alan was running up behind me as I climbed the brae to my house. 'Forget they tossers. They're just windin y'up.'

'You get fed up of it, night after night...'

'Aye. It's like Lila and me. I'm sure she only talks about that Big J because she knows it pisses me off. I mean, that's it isn't it?' He peered at me. 'You haven't heard anything else?'

'I've never even seen this Jye-guy.' I turned to look at the bay now all dark except for the Dounby light, long, short, fifteen seconds, long, short...

'I don't like it,' he said. 'Lila's talking now about changing her mind about the College. We were both supposed to be going to Edinburgh Uni. It's been planned for yonks. Now, she's talking about not being sure. It's all to do with this new guy.'

'That's just Lila. You ken what she's like.'

'Somebody must have put the idea in her head.'

'Maybe Shopsoiled Susan? She's never liked you.'

He pulled a face. 'It's Hecky she doesn't like. I don't think she's that bothered about me.'

'I wouldn't trust her. She's full of spite.'

In the next few days there were a lot of rumours about the party or the orgy or séance or whatever it was going to be. They were going to roast a sheep, dig up the corpse of old Mrs McRae who only died in March. They were going to have a massive gang-bang, they were going to steal a trawler and head for Spain. Whatever, it was going to be wild; that was all agreed on. Breeks ordered an extra supply from his dealer in Duncairn. We stockpiled cans and bottles in our special hiding places. I had already decided not to tell my parents about it. I'd simply sneak out of the house once they were in bed. Alan didn't have those kinds of problems. At that time of night, Hecky would be blootered somewhere, maybe on the floor of the public bar in the Norseman or asleep in the toilets of the Dounby Hotel. So – roll on Saturday.

We were to meet up in the car park, halfway up the brae, clear of the houses, at midnight. I didn't expect to see more than half a dozen when it came to it, despite the big talk. I called for Alan.

He came to the door. 'Robbie, I'm not going.'

'What? It'll be a hoot. Most likely nothing will really happen anyway.'

'Na, sorry and that. Do me a favour will you? Keep an eye out for Lila. Let me know what's going on with that new guy.'

'It'll be pitch black!'

'You ken what I mean.'

'You'd be better coming yourself.'

'I can't be bothered. The whole thing is daft. There's a cracking movie on anyway. Sly Stone.'

'What a crap-out! Well, I'm going anyway.'

'See you!'

The lights of the Norseman were flaring in the fog but there was no sign of anyone on the little lanes. I reached the steps and took them in twos. I heard a low whistle. Breeks emerged from a gable end. He flashed a penlight torch at my face.

'Just been having a pish,' he announced. 'In Mrs Mather's window boxes. See, I like to water her nasturtiums once a week.'

'Daft get! You only live down the way. You could use your own bog.'

'That's no the point. Where's Muiry?'

'No coming.'

'Probably studyin. His brain'll get soft!'

'Na, he's watching *Rambo II*,' I told him.

'Muiry's no coming? Magic!' Breeks exulted. 'I'll maybe get a grip of that wee Lila all to myself. Who's your babe?'

Since I didn't answer, he suddenly chuckled in the dark. 'Course, I forgot you're spoken for. Brung your lollipops – ye child-molester?' He shone the torch in my face.

I pushed him, tried to grab the torch. 'No you as well!'

He jumped away and chortled. 'She's a right fit wee bird though, eh? I'd like to see her a' oiled up. Eh? In her leather troosers.'

'Awa, ya peedo!

'Like I always say, Robbie, if you can't get a sixteen-year-old, have a threesome with twa eight-year-olds.'

'Funnee!'

'I'm right horny the night, man.'

'Aye? When're ye no?'

When we got to the car park we could hear voices in the dark and see the red dots of cigarettes. I looked back at the jumble of lights beneath us, the moon slipping out from under dark clouds and fog to shine on the watery horizon. There was a cold wind up here and it lifted bits of paper out of the wire wastebins, which flickered around. It was that time of night when you couldn't hear the sea at all.

'Who's that?' somebody wanted to know. Sounded like Ed.

'Robbie,' I said, flicking the torch on and up at my face, 'and Breeks is here.'

'Where's Alan?' Lila asked. Or it might have been Yvie. They sounded alike. I pointed the torch. It was Lila.

'He's no coming.'

'Muiry's crapped out!' someone said.

'Who's that?'

'Me. Who's you?'

'This is Big J,' the girl's voice said. 'The new guy.'

'Pleased to meet you.'

'Respect. Robbie – is it?'

'Robbie, yeah.'

Somebody lit an old-fashioned lantern and held it up.

'Ed. It's you. Thought it was.' His leather jacket reflected the shine.

Over by the dyke, somebody started to strum guitar chords. Then someone dropped a real eggy one in the dark.

'Breeks – was that you?'

'Ya minger!'

'You'll have the Bobby up here in a minute,' somebody groused.

'Aye, maybe the jobby bobby!'

'Ho ho ho! You're so helluva funnee!'

'Shusht!'

'Everybody's got to be real quiet,' Big J said. 'Keep that lantern down and put your torches off.' He had assumed a leadership role right away. He sounded pretty mature. I couldn't see him properly of course, just the shape of him. He looked taller than me.

'Are we all here?' Rob asked in a put-on woman's voice.

'Na – we're a' b-b-b-bonkers!' about a dozen voices chorussed.

'Who are we waitin on?'

'The lassies – Rachel's no here, nor Rae or any of them. And where's Catto? He said he was coming.'

'Ach, Catto! Probably still in the hoose playing with his train set.'

Because it was so dark, there wasn't much we could do but wait. One or two ring-pulls snapped as people began to drink their carryouts and the smell of a joint wafted around.

'Somebody's coming!' someone whispered hoarsely.

'Shust! Keep quiet everybody!'

Somebody whistled below us and we heard a stone click on the road. Down in the public bar of the Norseman or maybe the Dounby Hotel, there was a burst of laughter. The moon streaked the water far out to sea. I tried to see my hand in front of my face and couldn't. You know how black it gets. I could make out a blur against the moon though as my fist clenched around the soft rubber of my torch.

We heard an anxious whisper. 'Who's there? Ken you're there. Can smell yer dope.'

'That Breeks?'

'Aye, it wis him a'richt!'

'Na, I'm over here,' said Breeks.

Everyone relaxed. 'It's Joe Kydd – the barman at the Inn.'

'Wha's that with you, Joe?'

'Susy, and a couple of wee lassies, Heather and Rachel. There's more coming too.'

Another group came up and then we set off along the track that follows the clifftops round to Redstanes. As we walked out on the headland we could see the Dounby Head light ahead of us every fifteen seconds. We followed Big J's lantern, keeping close together, shining our torches at our feet. It seemed to me there were a couple of dozen of us at least. A big crowd. It was great to be out so late, gave you a feeling of liberation and I was already half-stoned anyway. I was glad I'd worn my fleecy, my sweat-shirt and two tee-shirts – and three pairs of socks inside my wellies – because it was bloody freezing.

Just before the cemetery, a small track leads westwards into a narrow cove and about halfway along is the old limekiln. I'd seen it many times though it wasn't the kind of place you would visit on your own in the dark. It was a huge stone buttress built into the slope of the cliffs and it had several large entrances, arched with brick and lots of air vent holes. It's pretty old, I suppose, somebody told me it was eighteenth century and of course, there are plenty of rumours about the place, like that it's haunted.

Mind you, there's a lot of old places round here and somebody's bound to have made up a story about them being haunted. The winter nights in Dounby can be long and boring. Especially if the sheep are not being responsive. Or the hotel's run out of beer.

When we got down on the flat, we could hear the sea on the shingle, hissing away and lots of funny bird noises that could've spooked us if we'd been alone. I bumped into someone who was pissing onto the shingle and dropped my torch.

'Watch yourself!'

'Sorry mate.' I had no idea who it was. But I found the torch again. Up ahead, I could see Big J's face for the first time as he held the lantern up. He was quite good-looking I thought, or at least I imagined the girls would think so. Neat sideburns, quite long hair, long eyelashes, dark-haired.

'Robbie,' he called, 'go and find the stash of brands.'

'Brands?'

'I left them in the entrance nearest the fence. Here's matches.'

'Okay.' I went to look. The grass was already damp from dew and was massively overgrown. I heard him saying, above the growing hilarity: 'There's no ghosties here. So if you feel a hand touching you, you know it's somebody mucking about...'

I looked back at the lantern and the crowd of faces, half-illuminated, that swirled around it. Why had I been selected to get the brands? And why, I wondered, had I accepted his authority without question?

I struggled up to the entrance of the limekiln and found the stash of wooden battens in a pile. They all had cloth wrapped around one end and stank of creosote. 'Got them!' I called. There was no reply. I picked one up and leaned it against the wall. It took loads of matches to get it going, and then it flared suddenly. I waved the brand a bit then used it to light another. They all came over then and I began to hand them out. It was like we were pagans having a ritual or something.

'Robbie, can I no get one?' Heather asked, pulling at my elbow.

'Course you can.'

'Gie's one, Robbie!'

'Ah, wait, eh!'

They were all grabbing at the brands. Big J's voice cut across the hubbub. 'Get back! There's plenty. Just wait your turn till Robbie gets them lit.'

The faces began to swarm and glow in the flames. There was a lot of mucking about and then we saw that Joe's girl, Susy, was wearing a long white sort of robe.

'She must have brung it wi her,' Ed said. 'Wow! Is she a flippin druid or what?'

'I heard that,' Susy said. 'I'm a white witch, actually.'

'Are you going to dance naked around the fire?' someone asked hopefully.

'Might do,' Susy said. 'But it's a bit parky the now.'

Torches were waving about all over the shoreline as everybody gathered up driftwood and lumps of seacoal and soon there was an excellent bonfire in front of the entrance of the limekiln. Some mankit old deckchairs had been found and others had hauled a log up from the shingle to use as a bench. Everyone was getting stuck into the drink, though I noticed no one was going inside the limekiln.

'Dead creepy in there,' Breeks said. 'All kinds of beasties, man. Bats, rats, corpses, ghoulies, man. Here, have a toke.'

When we were wee we'd used to play in those old limekilns that dotted the coastline. Massive, fort-like edifices cut into the cliffs where limestone was rendered, under intense heat, for use as fertiliser in the eighteenth century. Built of solid stone blocks, except for the entrance arches that were made of special small bricks. The entrance was narrow and led into a large vault, high ceilinged, from which several air vents protruded. There were secondary chambers leading to another entrance. The floors were powdered earth. They had a musty, earthy smell, as if the limekilners had tried to recreate ancient tombs. The roof of the kiln was thickly overgrown with grass and weeds and rabbits had burrowed all around. They were good places for the drinking and that because no one could see us, unless they were out in the bay of course. Or standing on the roof of the crypt at the cemetery – and if they were doing that, they were more of a danger to themselves than to us.

'Witch!' Big J called. 'Time for your magic.'

There was lots of cheers and shouts and vampire howls. 'Get em off!' Breeks roared and made a piercing whistle.

One of the little girls – a friend of Heather's maybe – brought forward a crystal ball and placed it on the ground. On closer inspection, it turned out to be a goldfish bowl. There were hoots of derision.

'Silence, unbelievers!' Susy hissed. And she waved some kind of a green sparkler and sparks flew. And the crystal ball, or goldfish bowl, had a kind of fluorescent light inside it.

'Raising the deid!' someone shouted.

'Mrs McRae! Helloooo, Mrs McRae – are you there…?'

Nobody was taking it seriously. Breeks handed me a joint. It was great to be out with the stars, the elusive moon hanging about behind clouds over the sea, and all my mates. Dounby wasn't so bad at that moment.

'I command the spirit of Jeemie the goldfish!' I heard Rob declaim.

'Better wi a guppy!'

'Stop mucking about!' Heather said. 'Come on, give the witch a chance! Robbie, you tell them...'

'I couldn't possibly... possibly...' I sniggered. Sniffed. 'Gainst my religion... do your worst, fiend!'

'You're stoned too!'

'I fear so, quinie.'

Some of us found a spot to lie down and watch the pathetic attempts of Susy and a small group to give their ritual some solemnity.

'Look at them,' said Ed. 'Like something out of that Tam O' Shanter.'

'That Susy's no wearin a bra...' Breeks said. 'I mean, you can tell. No?'

'Mucky wee sod!'

Big J came over and Breeks gave him a blast.

'Cheers!' He inhaled sharply and squatted down beside us. It was the first time I'd seen his face properly. 'We'd be better off inside the place,' he said. 'Warmer. The others are going in. Coming?'

'Aye, well... all right.'

'Bit of a damp squib, this, eh?' Ed complained. 'I mean, no nude dancing, no virgin sacrificing. And what about the gang-bang? We were promised a gang-bang.'

'Aye, we're supposed to be Vampire Invaders,' Stuart giggled. That was the name of their band. 'A little bit of pillagin and rapin's long overdue.'

'Come on, let's have a look!'

Because the entrance of the limekiln is so narrow, we had to file in carefully, holding our brands at knee height. The interior was huge and shadows wobbled. It was already warm and eerie. Voices echoed and mumbles leaped out at us loudly. It was dusty soil underfoot, like thick carpet. There had been a subsidence and a pile of rubble had tumbled out of one of the walls.

'It's no safe,' a voice quavered from the far side of the rubble.

There was growing unease. *Somethin's in here!'*

'Aye! Somethin... There is somethin!'

The dancing flames fixed in a pair of fierce red, unblinking eyes in the far corner.

'Hoarns! The Horn-ed One!' Breeks screamed, clawing his way backwards to get out. He'd started a mass panic as we fought to get out of the kiln. I was caught up in it. It was frantic. Once out, we scattered. Some stood on the foreshore backs to the bonfire and the brands stuck in the earth.

'Where's Big J?' someone shouted. 'Anyone seen Big J...'

'The Deil's got him!'

'Ach, awa ye go!' I jeered.

'There's nothin in there, man!' Rob said. 'It was just Breeks stoned out his nut.'

A brand appeared low-down at the entrance to the kiln. It was Big J – crouching and pulling – unwillingly, bucking against him, gouging at his hand – a very angry ram! In the bright light we saw it break free, cavort, buck at him one last time, then braying with a deep macho rasping tone, it charged outwards and was lost in the darkness. We were gobsmacked.

'The horned one!' Ed snorted sarcastically.

'Ye had to be there, man,' Breeks moaned. 'Aw – its staring een!'

We all broke out cheering and almost had heart attacks due to laughing so much. The hysteria lasted for ages. Someone broke the goldfish bowl on a stone, capering about and there was nearly a fight about it. We were in good spirits all the way home. Big J was the hero of the night. His wrestling in the dark with Auld Nick would go down in the legends of Dounby.

I got hell of course, the next day. Mum and my stepfather, John, glared at me when I came down for breakfast. 'That door was left on the latch all night!' Mum accused. 'Where were you?'

'Your Highers is only weeks away, Robbie,' said John, stirring his tea. 'Do you want to fail them all? Do you, boy? You're going the right way about it! Throwing your life away!' The usual tirade. They were right of course, but it didn't matter, as it doesn't at that age.

I suppose, thinking back, a large part of our conception of ourselves revolved around our attitude to dope. The herb was what separated us from the adult world of Dounby. It seems an extraordinarily petty thing but dope afforded us a certain cachet with the younger kids, just as swaggering into the Dounby Hotel or the Norseman did with the over-eighteens. We couldn't get into the public bars because they knew our birthdays to the exact day, so we had our own scene. Breeks was our main man – there was somebody he knew in Duncairn – but we all knew where we could buy an eighth or a quarter or even just a pound deal at the Academy. There was no shortage and sometimes we even smoked homegrown since Breeks knew a couple who grew plants hydroponically in a barn near Redstanes. Mostly, we chipped in for him to do the business a couple of times a week.

Of course, in the intervening decade a lot of less innocent chemicals have come and gone but dope was our narcotic of choice. We'd tried e's and amphetamines and acid but dope was easy and familiar and we were connoisseurs with all the patter of experts.

Breeks could, of course, have gone legally into the bar, since he was nearly nineteen but his parents were shunned and it was known they had criminal records. They were sometimes mentioned as 'gyppos' which was partly true.

They had foreign blood somewhere along the line and his real mother was English. In fact, I'd hardly ever seen his father and when I did he was drunk. My parents didn't want to know that Breeks was one of my friends. He had left school at sixteen and signed on by letter every fortnight since then. He'd done a couple of weeks' work in a supermarket at Duncairn but he was so poorly suited to the work – he didn't even *look* clean – that he'd been back signing on within a month. I never once saw him lose his temper, except the time Big Alasdair Murie's German shepherd ate a quarter ounce. That pissed him off all right. He mentioned the event at least three times a week, even though it had happened three years ago. Made a big impression on him, if not on the dog, which slept for two days solid but was unaffected. Breeks had insisted on taking the dog out every morning and night and inspecting its faeces with a fork but he never got it back. If you're wondering, he was called Breeks because it was his least appealing but most noteworthy feature. His were baggy, streaked, frayed, crudely patched, oil-stained, urine-impregnated and glistened around the spaver with old sperms. On their last legs – if you'll excuse the pun.

But the arrival of Big J seemed to diminish Breeks' status, for J was never short of a smoke himself. Where he got it from, or who his supplier was, we often speculated on. He constructed the most ornately twisted and smooth-smoking reefers you ever smoked. Which really stoned you out. He was a joint-rolling professional. Yet he seemed untainted by the mind-bogglingly boring details of the thing. Breeks for example could talk of little else, what he had, how much it had cost, what so and so had said about the last joint he'd rolled, where he was going to buy the next deal... Don't get me wrong, dope smoking is great but being with dope-smokers is less great. In short, maaaan, the scene is ultra-boring. Dope-heads are boring. In fact, dope sums them up. The word, like, as a descriptor. But Big J could take it or leave it. His eyes were on higher things. He was a poet, someone had told me. He plays the saxophone, someone else had said. He was in the Foreign Legion, man, honest, someone else had it. This had been rather contradicted by rumours that he had been a gigolo or a model for a swimwear catalogue. It was widely believed he had been in prison. There was also discussion about the woman who had arrived in the village with him who seemed to have disappeared.

'Maybe she's dead in the hoose?' Breeks speculated. 'Eh? Maybe he's done her in.'

'Ach, away!' Rob jeered. 'Why would he do that?'

Big J himself was oblique on such matters, even if approached directly. 'She, man,' he'd drawl... 'She has her own life... I don't question...'

In a small place like Dounby, everyone knows more or less everything there is to know about everyone else after a month or so, but the background of Big J seemed to grow more obscure with each passing week. He was an enigma, a sphinx, and a mystery man.

The week after the séance, I saw him sitting on his own in the Beach Café. I went in and sat with him. He barely looked up. There was something melancholy about him that made you see how such exotic rumours could start.

'Are you going to be staying in Dounby long?' I asked.

He replied with a kind of mumble that gave nothing away.

'I can't see how anyone would want to move here,' I said. 'Most of us want to move out – as soon as possible.'

He raised a quizzical eyebrow at that. 'Yeah? Nice place. In touch with its sense of its self.'

I was startled and baffled in equal measure. 'What?'

He didn't elaborate further.

'Mystery man,' I said. 'That's what they call you.'

He sniffed. 'That what you think, Robbie?'

'Well... you're a poet I heard.'

He smiled faintly, toying with the dregs of coffee in his yellow mug. 'That,' he agreed. 'And a pusher, preacher, prophet, pilgrim and a problem when I'm stoned.'

'Eh?'

'Song,' he explained, smiling sadly. 'And you, Robbie, what do you do?'

'I'm still at the Academy...'

'No, what do you *do*?'

'Well... I don't know.... how do you mean?'

'What are you?'

I pondered. 'Just me, I suppose.'

'Good answer,' he said stroking his sideburns. 'Being you is the best you can be.' And gave me that look. Sort of his blue eyes like sort of staring away in the distance, right through you. Then he grinned and he didn't look quite so lost.

Although I've said it already, it's worth repeating. I don't remember what first impressed me about Big J. He was impressive. Being darkly good-looking helped, being the kind of guy who was never flustered or stuck for a decision helped. He had an easy grace. His curly dark hair always looked casual, his sideburns always neat, he had no zits like the rest of us, always looked healthily tanned, wore denim shirts like they were meant to be worn. He was a 'well set-up young man' as the older folk around here would say. His clothes seemed to fit him perfectly. If this sounds like mystic shite – then it is. I know no other way to say it. He captivated me. Inside a week, I felt I would follow him to certain death in battle. We loved him utterly. I wanted to be with him all the time but I did not want to be sycophantic. Ohmygod, no! I wanted to be his equal and I was walking on eggshells in case I was going to blow it. He became our leader, no question, within a week. Breeks was cool about it, even Alan had to accept it, reluctantly. Looking back, it seems we'd never had as much fun as when he was there to lead us. Before Big J, we had been drifting, floundering, fumbling towards adulthood, but with him in our midst every conversation, every event had significance, seemed to have meaning. I don't know how he did it. You couldn't see how it was done. But it was.

* * *

The next day was bright and mild and I woke up full of thoughts about Xanthe and Tara and couldn't wait to get there on the pretext of cutting the grass. It'd been a week since I'd been there. When I came into the kitchen my mother was snipping flowers for the church. I looked into the alcove where John usually sat. She saw my glance. 'He's doing an extra shift at Croll's. Won't be back till teatime.'

'Good.' I made no pretence of liking him. I had resented him from the first, especially his religious mania, which seemed to me to be pure hypocrisy.

'Not a very nice thing to say,' she chided. 'Toast?'

I couldn't go up there too early. Once I'd finished my breakfast I sat in my room reading a book. *The Lord of the Rings.* I'd read it before of course. At 10am, I stood up but decided it was too early. It was gone ten-thirty before I sauntered up the hill. There were a couple of boats on the horizon and although it was difficult to tell, they looked like Gardyne boats. Turning in at the drive, I noticed that the Range Rover was gone. The bungalow looked empty. I was severely disappointed. I walked into the garden and looked over at the sea. Then I inspected the grass. It was tufty and overgrown. It occurred to me that Mrs Pritchard would be pleased if I had it cut by the time she got back. I dragged the mower out of the shed and filled the tank with petrol. Then I jerked the starter and it pulled me bumpily over the grass. I turned at the far end and came back towards the house. I happened to glance up, saw a face at the window and realised it was Oliver's niece. When I looked again, she was gone.

I couldn't think of any pretext to get inside the house. I didn't want to appear too eager. I took a break after about an hour and sat on the seat in the dell beneath the trees at the back of the shed and took out the joint I had been saving. I was savouring the swooning relaxation of it in my feet and fingertips when I heard footsteps.

'So what else is there to do around here except get stoned?'

'What?' I started and jumped to my feet. Tara Compton stood at the stone steps; her cropped blonde head tilted teasingly in my direction.

'Like, you must be the grass-master?' she said, left hand poised on her hip. She wore tight faded jeans whose waistband had been cut off. There were slashes above each knee through which her brown legs could be seen. A white sleeveless tee-shirt barely covered her belly button. I saw freckles on her shoulders. Then the ghetto blaster in her other hand roared into life: *her name is Rio and she dances in the sand...*

'You like the New Romantics?' she suddenly asked. 'I think they're cool.'

'Yeah, they're um...'

'Are you ever going to give me a puff of that?' she asked, holding out her hand.

'Sure. It's Tara, isn't it?'

'Right.'

'Oliver's niece?'

'Right.' She came and sat beside me on the bench. 'Good grass,' she said after a moment or two. 'Is this all you've got?'

'I can get more.'

'You're Robert?'

'Robbie,' I corrected.

'Cool. You still at school?'

I told her I was nearly finished with school but that I planned to go to University.

'College? I'm going to go to College. I'm taking a year out. My parents are against it but I couldn't face another year of studying just yet. That's why I'm here. So, like, do a lot of kids around here smoke?'

'Everybody.'

'Cool. It's dead boring when you don't know anybody.'

I smiled at her. 'Great.'

She looked at me crossly. 'That's funny?'

'I was hoping you'd say that,' I explained. 'Because maybe you'd want to come for a walk.'

'Sure.' She sniffed. 'Could you maybe get me some?'

'Oh, yeah. Loads.'

'Well, I have to go now,' she said. 'Are you coming up tomorrow?'

I waited for a few moments then looked at her. 'Yeah, I could.'

'Well, I'll see you then.'

'See you.'

4

Because Dounby is hemmed in by the cliffs and sea, it can be like a prison, which is why in the olden times smugglers found it a good bolthole. Sometimes I just wanted to get away. Dounby was like the arse-end of the universe. It was worse with the exams only a fortnight away and the parents making me stay in all the time. But the weekends – they had to let us out to get some air – were free. The weather was turning better too, so now we didn't have to spend so long hanging around inside the Beach Café, enduring Sandy Stokes' blethers. We could sit on the wall outside the sheds at the Old Landing and chill, just watching the beach, doing nothing except maybe toss the occasional crab claw or pebble at the (non-existent) tourists picking their way over the shingle to go and gawp at the Maiden Stane. Using an old biro to fire barley seeds was another old trick, if they came within range. So we were practising. Or talking about practising. Unless there were tourist girls of our age about, then we'd have something to do – but that almost never happened. The tourist season hadn't got going yet. The caravan park at Gardyne would open in a couple of days. You never knew if there would be any girls there. It's good to have new faces around the place, even if it's just tourists. Of course, I didn't say anything about Tara. I wanted to keep her to myself.

Shopsoiled Susan, the gnarled manageress of the Shoprite, glared at me like she was part of the project to clone me and wanted to make sure every detail was exact. She's a nosy cow: suspects me of shoplifting which I haven't done for months anyway and even then it was only the odd Mars bar when Yvie's back was turned. Yvie was using the big ray-gun thing for pricing cans. She was standing on a little ladder to get to the top shelf stuff and I could get a look at her legs because she had on her school skirt under the daft green nylon jacket they make her wear. I could feel Shopsoiled's peepers boring holes in my back so I just got a packet of hula-hoops and a can of Irn Bru and beat it out of there. Shopsoiled's teeth were yellow and nicotine-stained and stuck out at different angles. Even when I'd got my change and was out of the shop I could feel her staring.

When I got past the old jetty to the Old Landing, there was only Breeks and Ed there, practising their farting skills.

'Sit on the oil drum like this—' Breeks was explaining, 'see, astride it but no making it fold over... dinna bend it. Spread yer erse wide so that yer bumhole is right down on the drum like... see!'

While Ed and I gazed critically, he let out a ripper that reverberated dully inside the empty drum.

'Brilliant!' Ed said. 'I'll have a go.'

I sat looking out at the same old greasy water, nothing to see except the sea. The horizon was like invisible bars of the jail.

'You no wanting to try it?' Ed asked after a few goes.

'No,' I said without interest. 'But you carry on. Enjoy yourselves!'

'What's wrong wi him?' Breeks asked.

'Owre much studyin. It's softened his brains.' Ed looked over at me. 'Hey, Prof, what's the formula for a ketone?'

'Piss off!'

Breeks' wind instrument bassooned loudly. 'Aw! That was a guid ane! D'you hear that?'

'I can dae better, man!'

I went up for Alan. I rang the bell for a long while. I guessed he was still in bed but I heard him shouting through the toilet window.

'That you, Robbie?' His voice sounded bleary. 'What's up?'

'Coming down to the Coble Landing? You still in bed?'

'Ah, no. I'm crappin man. On the bog.'

'I can hear you!'

'What?'

'Never mind.'

'Fish curry last night. One of Hecky's specials. This is my third crap since I woke up. Don't come in for a while.'

'You coming out?'

'Hold on. That curry was wicked. I need a few more shites man, before I'm straight. Give me five.'

Back on the Landing, the farting contest had mutated into a belching contest.

'See, if you belch into the drum...' Ed explained.

'I can't hear nothing,' Breeks derided. 'You'll need to make another hole. Here's what to do, man... bore a wee hole in the side and belch into it...'

They experimented for a while. Alan and I watched.

'Hud your hand over the nozzle...'

'Better with something, maybe paper, over the nozzle.'

'Pit baith the drums thegither... mair echo...'

Breeks roared in annoyance and stood up accusingly. 'Aw, stuff it, ah've ile a' owre ma fizzer!'

'Ye look like someone who's escaped from the Black and White Minstrels!' Alan jeered.

Breeks held out his hand. 'Got a hankie on yous?'

'What! I'm no gettin it oily! Use the hem of yer teeshirt.'

Breeks' eyebrows met in the middle of his forehead, the sign of sudden thought. 'Wait, ah could use sand! Like the Airabs.' He ran off, at the half-crouch.

'He's a daft nickums,' Ed said. 'Look at him washing his face with the sand.'

'Like a sort of gibbon,' Alan agreed, 'some kind of an ape anyway.'

We watched him for a while. We could hear him shouting to himself: 'This is really braw!'

'So, you guys do any more practising?'

'Na,' Ed explained. 'The Vampire Invaders are off the road the now. If only we could get oor amplifiers back. We're going into the school later for a practice. Fancy coming?'

'Village Bobby still no giving them back? That's pure total fascism!'

'Well,' Ed groused, 'my mum's put in a complaint to the police at Duncairn about it. Mind, that was two weeks ago and I've heard nothing.'

'Here's Big J coming!'

We watched him approach, kicking at the loose shingle with his Doc Martens, hands bunched inside the pockets of his bikers' jacket.

'What does the J stand for?' Alan asked.

'Dunno. Probably Jimmy or Joe maybe. Ask him.'

'Hi, Big J guy.'

He gave us a lopsided smile and rummaged in the curly hair at the back of his head. 'Why's that loon, Breeks, lying on his face?'

'Because of the oil.'

His eyes opened wider. 'Struck oil? On the beach?'

'Oil on his face.'

'Next time, I won't ask.' He found himself a niche against the wallboards in the shade and flipped a mouth organ out of his top pocket.

Ed began to whistle along. It was the Eurythmics.

Breeks came thundering up. 'Got it all off... can yous see any oil on my puss?'

'Guys,' Big J said, ruminatively, looking at his mouth organ. 'Know anything about a pair of blondes I seen earlier outside the Norseman?'

'Oh yeah!' we chorused.

'That'll be Nikki and her sister, Loren,' I explained. 'They just started on Thursday. Loren's the barmaid and Nikki works as a waitress. They're here for the season. You not seen them before?'

'Nope. So, any of you guys...?'

We just gaped at him. 'What! They're... Nikki is twenty-one and Loren is even older. Finnish – from Finland.'

Ed tried to do the voice: 'Ve coomin froom Finloond yah? *Ve like to snog many Scottish men, is so?* Oiky va.'

'They speak English?' J drawled, then answered himself. 'Must do, working there. And none of you guys...?'

We shook our heads. 'None.'

'They share a room on the third floor at the back,' Ed told him.

'We tried everything, man,' Breeks explained. 'Borried a ladder, climbed the hill, tried to use Stuart's dad's binoculars...'

Big J shook his head. He looked sorrowfully at the mouth organ, and then played a few notes. 'Peeping? Voyeurism? Not my scene.' He clicked his tongue in disapproval and shook the spittle out the mouth organ and put it in his top pocket. 'Bad karma, lads, makes you blind. So which is which?'

'Loren's the tall, thin one...' I said. 'She's the nicest...'

'Least you talked to her then?'

'Oh, yes, talked, yes...'

'So Nikki is the busty one, huh? Well guys, I don't want to cramp your style but let me tell you today is the first day of the open season for beaver!'

Breeks blew a long whistle. 'Which one you fancy, Big J?'

J slowly turned and grinned. 'Now, Breeks, never play favourites. Specially when they're sisters. Have they got a car at all?'

'No,' Ed said. 'Seen them getting the bus.'

'But you don't have a car either, J?' I said, frowning.

He looked at me with that slow-spreading grin. 'I've got a motorbike, Robbie, which is the next best thing. How are you getting on with the folks up at the bungalow?' I knew he meant Mrs Pritchard.

'All right. I don't like the guy she's brought with her. That Oliver.'

He laughed. 'That's all right. She doesn't either.'

I was about to ask what he meant by that when he got to his feet and stroked his left hand through the longish hair at his temple. 'Got to go,' he said mysteriously. A few steps further, he half-turned. 'Beaver season!' he called, winked, and strode away, whistling.

'Wahey!' Breeks said. 'He means to have them both.'

Alan snorted. 'They're too sophisticated to fall for that aw-shucks Texan routine,' he said. 'D'you notice by the way he wears a ring on his little finger? I never saw that before. A sort of diamond.'

'That chain around his neck has got to be gold,' Ed said. 'I heard that he's been knocking off Yvie.'

There was an appalled silence.

'Naw? Kidding? Yvie? God!'

'That's bullshit!' Alan said reddening. 'Absolute bullshit! Just a dirty rumour. Yvie doesn't fancy him. She said he was like some kind of oily truck-driving Elvis clone. Which he is.'

'Yeah... but...' Ed reasoned. 'They just live across from him and he's in that flat on his own. Dead easy to nip in for a quick one.' He winked at me.

'Ach, Lila wouldn't let her!' Alan argued. 'Lila would tell me and spread it all over the place.'

'Maybe he's having them both?' Breeks suggested, with a dirty laugh. 'Threesomes! Said he liked them in pairs.'

'Watch it, you!' Alan threatened, chasing Breeks away with a bit of wood. 'Gerroutof it, ya gibbon!'

'Nah, not them pair,' Ed said quietly to me as we watched Alan pursuing Breeks along the shingle. 'I think J's got someone else, anyway.'

'Yeah? Poor Alan... he's not letting Breeks off with it,' I said. 'Look. But Lila's giving him the run-around. She's not going with him to Edinburgh in October.'

'Nah? That's been on the cards a long time.'

'We'll ask the lassies what they think,' I said, nodding at the girls who were coming out by the jetty. 'They're bound to have all the latest goss.' I could see Heather, Rachel and a couple of thirteen-year-olds. Alan joined them, giving up on the chase.

'Fancy a ride?' Breeks shouted through his cupped hands from the shingle.

'Get lost!' Rachel shouted back at him. 'He's disgusting,' she said, coming up to us. 'Just a dirty-minded little tink.'

Heather said. 'Haven't seen you for a while, Robbie, been hiding from us?'

'Nah,' I said, thinking about Tara Compton. 'Course not.'

She sat down beside me and crossed her legs. Fourteen going on forty double-d. She offered me a lick at her Kia-Ora.

As I leaned over to lick it, I saw the shape of her breast outlined by the sun in the cotton tee-shirt. We were all growing up. I hunched forward as if I was fascinated by the crummy lobster pots under the wall.

'I've been saving my cherry for you,' she said.

I stared at her. 'What?'

She nodded at the lollipop. 'Cherry,' she said. 'My favourite.'

'Oh right.'

'Saw that Big J earlier,' she said. 'You know he's been visiting those Pritchards at the house on the hill?'

I looked at her in amazement. 'What? He never said.' I glanced over at Alan chatting to Rachel and Ed. 'Why would he be going there?'

'I don't know. You know them too, don't you? Same reason as you. Rachel's aunty has been taken on to do a bit of cleaning,' Heather told me. 'The woman that's rented it has a kind of forge.' She thought for a moment. 'You know... sort of forge... oxy...'

'Oxy-acetylene?'

'Yeah that's it, like she's welding metal or something. In the shed.'

'Why would she be doing that?' Alan asked. I said nothing.

'I don't know, do I? But Rachel's aunty has seen it.'

'Heather, don't embarrass the laddie!' Rachel called over. 'I don't believe J's doing anything with those barmaids – or Yvie.'

'With *who*?' Alan shouted, red-faced.

'Nobody. Just teasing,' Rachel smirked.

'We got to go,' Ed said. 'You coming, Robbie?'

Breeks ran after us on the beach. 'Where are you going?' he asked. 'Can I come?'

'My dad's giving us a lift into the school,' Ed said. 'Band practice. Robbie said he would give us a hand with the stuff.'

'I'll give you a hand too!' Breeks offered.

Ed and I looked at each other.

'He's no sittin wi us!' Rachel shouted. 'Tinky minger.'

'All right,' Ed said. 'You can come, but don't mention anything about dope. My dad knows what it smells like. He's not daft.'

'They let you practise at the school?' Heather asked. She had tagged along behind us.

'Yeah, Mr Salmond the music teacher has to be there to let us in.'

'They're doing a gig at the Gardyne flower show,' I said. 'We'll expect all the groupies to be there.'

'We're not groupies!' Heather said, miffed. 'But we wouldn't miss it. What are you going to do about your amplifiers?'

Ed sighed. 'Village Bobby has to let us have them back by then. It's doing my head in not having them.'

'See you later, lover!' Heather teased, blowing kisses at me when we reached the concrete walkway at the Seatown.

'She fancies you mate,' Breeks said. 'Better get in there, or I'll ride it myself.'

'You couldn't get anywhere near Heather Lowdy!'

'Oh yeah? Watch me. See, they get that randy at that age... they don't care who they go with... anything in trousers, man. Frustration...'

'Bullshite!'

Although I've never been musical, I liked hanging round with Ed, Stuart and Rob. I didn't know the drummer Josh, a fifteen-year-old who lived in Gardyne. The Vampire Invaders was a pretty crass name, and, to be honest, they weren't terribly inventive. Loud – that was the best thing about them. Which is why Village Bobby had impounded their amps after lots of complaints. Mostly, they just did cover versions of heavy metal classics that everybody could head-bang along to. They had a reputation too after trouble erupted at a party they were playing at in Redstanes. Some Goth chicks used to turn up, all purple and black lipstick, pretty weird. My chances of scoring were definitely higher if I hung around with the band. I wondered whether Tara would be interested. Trouble was, maybe she'd lose interest in me and fancy Rob instead.

'Look, Breeks man, there's no space in the van, sorry and that.' Ed said. 'See, my dad's got all this building stuff in it. And we've got to pick up Josh and his drum-kit. I forgot about that.'

'Sorry, man,' Rob said firmly. 'It's no possible.'

'I'm not that bothered either,' I offered.

'That's okay, Robbie,' Rob said. In an undertone, he added, 'We'll be going for a pint later, if you're up for it.'

'Ah well,' Breeks said, unabashed. 'I'll head back to the shed, see if that Heather's still up for a shag.' He grinned in my direction to see if I was bothered.

'Please yourself,' I said.

'Daft nickums!' Ed said. 'I didn't want him coming along. He's banned from the school ye know.'

'I didn't.'

'Oh yes, last year – don't you remember? – he was caught with some lassie in the toilets. Thirteen. He was lucky he didn't get the jail. Especially with all this hoohah about peedies.'

'Yeah, Breeks is nineteen, I keep forgetting.'

'Whoops, here's my dad. Keep shtum!'

Rob, Stuart and Ed loaded their stuff in the back of the white Transit alongside sacks of cement, hods and trowels. Jim McGugan looked at me but said nothing, kept scratching at his stubbly brown and white beard. 'In the front, lads,' he ordered. 'Robbie and the other lad will have to go in the back.'

The Transit had a sofa seat so you could fit three up front plus the driver. I had to sit behind them, on a rough pallet, wedged against the seatback. We began to crawl up the winding road out of Dounby so slowly I thought it would start to slide back. I could see the harbour dropping out of the rear windows. Jim cursed and had to stick in first.

'A' this cement,' he explained, puffing smoke at the windscreen. 'Should have dumped it at the works yesterday.'

I was looking forward to promised driving lessons once my exams were over and keenly watched the way Jim used his gears, and imagined I was steering round the bends. It looked dead easy. But I'd want a vehicle with a little more class. The drummer, Josh, was waiting at the top of the road down to Gardyne. The wind was scattering the blue-green water, darkening its stripes. A couple of fishing smacks, trailing white and spiralling seagulls, disappeared under the cliffs, heading for the harbour.

Josh was a lanky, languid youth sitting on the dyke beside the bus shelter, puffing away at a fag like an old man.

Ed's dad pulled up for him.

'Heh – where's a' your gear?' Rob asked in concern.

'Salmond says I can use the school kit.'

'Oh. Right.'

'Laddie – you'll need to get in the side door,' Jim McGugan told him. 'Sit on one of the pallets.'

It wasn't brilliant to be going into school on a Saturday. The place was empty and smelt fresh – for once. No sweaty feet or stinky knickers of small-fry sperms. When we reached the music rooms that were next to the big gym, a group of young girls came out with violins and cellos. We made room for them to pass and eyed them hungrily, like... well, like vampire invaders.

'Right, you boys!' Mr Salmond appeared in the corridor. He was the burly type, heavy with mad black eyes and floppy hair. 'Chop chop! You've only got an hour and twenty minutes.' He glared at me. 'You, boy, what do you play?'

'He does rhythm,' Ed told him, adding in an undertone, 'the rhythm method...'

'Right, where's your instrument? Get it out then, boy!'

'You said I could use the school drum-kit,' Josh said.

'You'll have to put it together. The cymbals are next door and the hi-hats.'

Josh clicked his tongue in annoyance and Salmond rounded on him like a poisonous adder. 'Think you're Ringo Starr, do you, eh?' he shouted. 'You use it, you put it up, you take it down when you're finished.'

'Ringo who?' Josh pouted.

Salmond fixed him with a fishy glare. 'Right, now, I'll be in Music Room 1, just along the corridor,' he said, 'so watch the decibels, eh?' He turned at the door. 'Not having any repetition of last time, or this is your last practice, yes?'

'Yes,' we chorused.

When he had gone and after a couple of trips to the next room to collect the rest of the drum-kit, Ed locked the door. He unzipped his case and brought out his imitation Stratocaster, wiping along the fretboard with a hanky.

BOOMP BOOMP BOOMP WHARRUMPA BOOMP BOOMP BOOMP BAROOMPA BOOMP went Stuart's bass.

'Jesus! Too loud!' Ed screamed. 'Down, down... or we'll have The Fish back in here.'

'Sorry!'

Boomp boomp boomp wharrumpha boomp boomp boomp...

Neowwhhh.... whang whungggg gungg guh...! screamed feedback from Ed's guitar as he stood too near the amp.

Josh tested the footpedal: Dumpha dumpha dumph-dumph, then struck the hi-hat: tshum ... tssstt ... shtt ... shoo!

'Ready?'

I put my feet up on a desk but truth to tell, I was sitting with Tara on the bench at the Pritchard's place.

* * *

I was eating breakfast next morning when there was a knock at the back door. John called from the hall. 'Someone for you, Robert.' It was Big J, hunched forward, hands thrust deep in his pockets.

'Hi, Robbie.' He glanced at the toast in my hand. 'Fancy a stroll?'

'Eh, right. I'll get my jacket.'

We walked along the street out to the Braeheid and stopped by the door of his flat. He patted the green canvas canopy that covered his motorbike. 'Fancy a hurl?'

'Oh, yeah!'

'Just along the coast road,' he looked at me quizzically, 'maybe as far as Duncairn?'

'Great.'

Hands in my pockets, I stood and watched him strip the cover off the bike. 'I wanted to speak to you about Mrs Pritchard,' he said quietly.

'Mrs Pritchard? You mean...?'

'Yeah.'

'Actually, I heard you knew them.'

Now it was his turn to look surprised. He grabbed my arm. 'Who told you that, Robbie? Who?'

'Can't remember. I'm surprised you didn't say before.'

'Okay.' He handed me the spare helmet. 'Look, if I tell you, you've got to promise me to keep it to yourself.'

I felt honoured that he trusted me with his secrets. 'Okay.'

'Mrs Pritchard – Xanthe –' he paused, examining the interior of his helmet. 'I was on my bike up on the main road and I saw her walking,' he said slowly. 'She waved, you know. I stopped. I thought she was... some problem. She said she wanted to have a ride on my bike. You know, she sort of smiled. Well, you know...'

'So?'

'So, I'm seeing her. When he – Oliver – isn't there.' He stroked the petrol tank cover shyly. 'I think she likes me.'

'My God!'

'Yeah!' He put on his helmet and snapped the chinstrap. 'I know she's friends with you. She told me. Thing is I've never met anyone like her. I knew her before, you know.'

I stopped in the act of putting on the helmet. 'When?'

He seemed distracted. 'When...? Down in Glasgow. I used to know some art students. She had an exhibition.'

I took a deep breath. 'So you're...?'

'No, Robbie. We just chat. I've only been there twice. I thought I'd be... I mean it looked like she wanted...'

A sudden anxiety struck me. 'When you go there... is Tara there?'

'Oliver's wee niece? No, of course not.' He sat astride the bike. 'Get on,' he said. 'Tara's only fifteen you know. You want to watch it. You could get done for statutory rape if you go with her.'

'What?'

He revved the engine. 'Fifteen.'

'She's sixteen.'

'Xanthe told me.'

'What?'

I couldn't hear the rest. He turned the bike in a wide arc and we were off up the hill with a load roar. I could see a few curtains twitching.

It was a clear open day, quite windy when we got to the upper road, the B8760. The road swerves and undulates along the coast. You go down into deep valleys and crest the tops of high hills with panoramic views of the sea. I kept a tight grip of J's waist but soon relaxed and got into the way of leaning in or out with the bike as it swerved. The countryside raced past in a green blur. Soon we were on the outskirts of Duncairn. Big J beat the lights and took us out onto the links and down by the wide sands. He slowed and parked outside a café on the Esplanade. I stepped off the bike and felt a little dizzy. I was troubled by what he had told me. We got the window table in the café behind the perspex flysheet, stained and blotched with last season's victims.

The coffee in the plastic cup was too hot to drink, microwaved. 'That Oliver's a slimy bastard anyway,' I said. 'Two weeks ago he insisted on taking me into town. I thought it was just to go shopping or have a look about. He took me into a bar on the docks. A hoors' place. The Mandrake. Then believe it or not up to a flat in the old town to visit a prostitute.'

J rubbed the damp hair behind his ear. 'Oliver did? He went with a pro? You're kidding me?'

I stared into my cup, 'It's what happened. He wanted me to go with her and all. But there was no way! Although she seemed nice.'

He sipped his coffee, both hands around the mug and looked at me over it. 'Well... what a dirty bugger! And to think he shares Xanthe's bed every night! You sure this woman was a prostitute? Can't believe he would take you to see her – and then go with her – with you there? Like, does he expect you not to tell on him?'

'He warned me not to. He knows I can't. Mrs P would never believe me over him.'

'Yeah, I suppose. And this woman was young?'

'Not that young.'

'And he definitely paid her?' he inquired. 'I mean you saw that? Or is this not just a woman he knows, this Tish, like a regular girlfriend.'

'Maybe. He did seem to know her.'

He smiled. 'I never would have suspected Oliver. Mind you, he is an ugly brute. What a loser though, eh? Paying for it.'

'I don't think he treated her well, either. I had the impression he was hitting her or something.' I told him more detail about what I'd seen and what I suspected Oliver had got up to. J listened, nodding, and made no comment.

We strolled along the front for a while. It was windy and cold. There wasn't a single person on the beach. There were hardly any people on the prom either.

'So you and Tara, I take it, haven't done the deed?'

I was aghast. 'Oh God no!'

'Good. Better check her birthday date first, my advice. So does this mean you're a novice at the bonking, Robbie?'

I turned away and looked out to sea. 'Oh, I've had loads of girls... but I've never... gone all the way. It's a small place, Dounby.'

'But in touch with its sense of itself!' Big J laughed. 'Look, why don't you show me where this woman lives.' He sniffed. 'Let's have a look at her place. You never know, Oliver might be there now. We could catch him in the act, pants down.'

'And then what?'

'Then he might go back to where he came from.'

It occurred to me that if that happened, Tara would be gone too. 'All right,' I said reluctantly. 'I'll show you. Just for a look. We're not going to speak to her or anything.'

'Of course not. We don't want anyone to know that we know. Knowledge is power.'

But once we were parked outside the house, Big J then decided we should at least check the name on the door. 'She doesn't know anything about me,' he said. 'Keep your helmet on. I'll just ask her for directions. Try to suss out the situation.' He swung his legs over and removed his helmet.

He stood at the cottage door. My stomach was churning. He knocked again. Then he sauntered back to the bike.

'No one here,' he said. 'Waste of time. Let's go.'

Just as he got back on the motorbike, a car came along quite fast and pulled in to the kerb in front of us. A man got out and looked – glared – but didn't speak. He went up the path to the door and then hesitated in front of it. J spoke out of the corner of his mouth. 'Another disappointed punter.'

'No,' I whispered. 'It's the husband.'

'M. Jorgenssen,' J said. 'Unless that's just her name.'

But just then the door was opened from the inside and the man went in, but I could see him watching us from the doorway as the bike pulled away.

* * *

I'd done a lot of thinking about what I wanted to do when school was behind me. It didn't involve Dounby. There was no future in the place, unless you wanted to eke out a living in boats of one sort or another – and I didn't. Until ten years ago, that was what all the lads of the village did.

No one was expected to go on to Higher Education. But the village had changed a lot – there were a lot of incomers. My parents were incomers. Came to Dounby because of their religion. True. My father and mother met and married in a Mission station of the Church of the Second Chance and that was why they ended up going to Dounby. Most of the village is unhealthily obsessed with God. The Gospel Hall is fair packed on a Sunday, as is the Jehovah Meeting House and the Church of Scotland over at Gardyne. Some of the villagers walk over there every Sunday in their Sunday best and wellies. The Adventists, the United Frees and the Baptists have meeting rooms here too and the Episcopalians have a travelling caravan that visits every month but religion bores me rigid so if you want to know more you'll have to get someone else to tell you about it. Anyway, up until ten years ago in Dounby there was, apparently, a universal expectation that people would play down any public display of differences. There was a modesty that came from so many people living jammed so close together. Having a son or daughter go off to College would have been seen as outrageously immodest, a kind of bragging. The sort of thing your family could never live down, but then, of course, there was plenty well-paid work on the doorstep at the fishing. But things have changed. The fishing industry's on its last legs and the village is not nearly as claustrophobic as it used to be either. Tension between the 'auld-yins' and the 'incomers' still breaks out now and then of course. Our group being mostly kids of incomers, we mostly live in the council housing halfway up the hill and most of us intend to stay on at the school. Then we're all going to break out. For some of the 'auld yins' this is treachery. Not that they'd tell you as much to your face. Like Hecky, he can't understand us at all. It's mutual. For his part, Alan often says he's the first Homo sapiens in the family, thinks of Hecky as a Neanderthal. My folks are always on at me about coming to the Gospel Hall and trying to interest me in some frumpy girl or other who's some church elder's daughter and just wants to be a fisherman's wife. I probably forgot to mention – my stepfather works at a fish-processing factory – Croll's – in Duncairn and mum works part-time at the village sub post office. Well, they have done for five years since we came to Dounby although they were now having a running battle over the subject of Sunday collections to which they are devoutly opposed. Most of the incomers think it's a good idea of course and nowadays they're – we're – in the majority. Personally, who cares if they collect letters on a Sunday? I don't. Some people should get a life!

So our crowd are black outsiders, rebelling against our incomer parents who are in a sort of rebellion themselves against the auld yins. And Big J? He was an outsider even to our group, an incomer among incomers. There was something that marked him out. But I'm getting ahead of myself. It was an afternoon in June. The exams were finally over. After I handed in my papers for my last one, Higher English, I played football in the playground with a furious intensity, scuffling on the tarmac for the tennis ball with my peers and I scored many magical goals. It was a mega-triumph. I was held head high by the cheering fans to the dressing rooms and invited to become Club Chairman and player manager of the Scotland World Cup squad. Then we got on the bus, pushing and shoving as usual to get next to the Gardyne girls at the back. It was noisy and everyone was trying to show off. You'd think they'd be fed up of doing that, day in day out for whole terms. I sat beside Alan and sang silently to myself on the way home, exulting at every clifftop vista from Scuggie Ness to the Lang Rock, thinking about how soon it was just going to be a memory.

'I feel sure I've done well enough to pass,' I kept saying.

'No bother. Anyway, best thing is to forget all about it now.'

'Don't worry. Forget about what?'

'I'm not going in next week,' he said. 'You?'

'Nah. Going to the party though.'

'Course. The party. I'm still trying to arrange a crash-pad for after.'

I made a face. 'There's just no way my folks would allow that. Anyway, it finishes at midnight. And there's buses arranged for the country folk.'

'Yuugh! That's for the poor sods who don't get off with anyone.'

'Good point. I'll have to think about it.'

The bus did its tight turn outside the Spar and let us off at the end of our street before heading back to the main road and all points west to Redstanes.

'See you at the café later, Robbie?'

I felt that my life was on track. No more Mr Schoolboy. There was a warm sun hovering over Dounby Head although when I got home the house was fully in shadow.

'How did it go, the exam?' Mum asked, peeling potatoes.

'What she means,' said John, 'is did you pass?'

I muttered something rude under my breath that they didn't catch.

'What?' said my stepfather sharply. 'Wash your mouth out!'

I stared down at him as if he was totally mad. 'I said,' I stated with dignity, 'how should I know? The results won't be out for six weeks at least. What? Am I meant to be a mind-reader now?'

'Insolent boy!' John raged. 'The sooner you leave home to whatever it is you want to do – the better.'

'Don't fight with your stepfather!' Mum called from the kitchen. 'Where's your respect?'

'Well, it was a stupid question. Anyway, the exam went well. But that's only what I *think*.'

My stepfather clicked his teeth in annoyance. 'How couldn't you have said that earlier, boy? That's all we wanted to know. Not this other nonsense about mind reading. You try my patience, boy. Sorely. I regret not chastising you more when you were younger.'

I didn't wait to hear any more but as I went up the stairs, I heard the unmistakable sounds of the leather-bound bible being taken down from the shelf.

'He is a trial to me, mother,' I heard him saying. He calls my mum mother. That is odd because he's fifteen years older than she is. He calls me boy as if he can't remember my name. I plugged myself into my CD player. Gustav Mahler. Symphony No 4 in G Major. Nobody knows I listen to this kind of stuff. I even amaze myself with it. Like, it hasn't got a beat, but it's fabulous, soars in your brain sort of. I saw the guy's face – Mahler – in some book and I thought 'What a speccy ponce.' But the 4th Symphony is really cool. Except the singing at the end. That makes me cringe. Anyway, it makes you think, music like that. You can lie with your eyes closed and let your mind wander far away from Dounby.

In the Beach Café later, there was a poor turnout. Some of the others still had exams ahead, O-grades. Yvie and Lila and Rob Lowdy were at home studying. Stuart and Ed were away buying an amplifier at Redstanes. Raymond Catto was there, unfortunately. I usually avoid him because even though he's in my year, he's just totally uncool. His parents are friends with mine – another reason to despise him. He was sitting in the corner; impossible to ignore the fat slug with his greasy white face and the short, almost shaved head that made him look as if at seventeen he was already balding.

'Exam was piss easy wasn't it?' he said. 'Pure dead easy. Didn't even have to switch on my brain box once. It was so easy it was just pure boring. I wish it had been more difficult. Don't you?'

'Get lost, Raymondo!' I snarled. 'What are you doing here anyway? Slumming it, I suppose?'

'Oh yeah.' He puffed himself up. 'Next week I'll be on a beach in Tenerife with my cousin Nick and his girlfriend Sandra. I'll be glad to get out of this place.'

'Bully for you.'

'No, really, Strachan, does you good to get away. Forget about the exams until the results come in. I expect five A's and a B. That's for Geography because I only did four questions. Not my fault. The String Bean should have told us to turn over the exam paper...'

I laughed like a hyena until he began to get annoyed.

'Not my fault at all. You'll see how well I've done when the results come down. Bet you. Five A's. Like to put money on it?'

'I couldn't be bothered. Catto, why don't you go and get an early start on your packing?'

I had been in a good mood until the Catto episode. Thankfully, he took the hint and wandered off. I sat by myself for ten minutes. Sandy Stokes was sitting up at the counter reading a newspaper spread in front of him. It was the kind with naked women on most of the pages. I could almost see his lips move as he read the words: 'Cindi loves badminton, flower-arranging and keep fit...'

'How's the motor, Sandy?'

He barely looked up. 'Coming along. Out for a trial any day now.'

Alan looked in. He winked at me and jerked his thumb over his shoulder.

'Got to go,' I said. 'Thanks.'

'Any day now,' Sandy said, peering closer at the newspaper page.

* * *

Right from the start when I met Tara by arrangement, it didn't feel remotely like a date. It wasn't like she was unattractive. She was, kind of, but there was something remote, detached and a little smug about her. I did fancy her a bit but I could feel her looking at me as if I was an oddity, one of the local youths she was slumming with just to prove she could. As if she was just killing time with me till she was ready to return to the real world.

'Oliver's my dad's younger brother,' she explained as we turned off from the Braeheid onto the sheep track that wanders along the cliff towards Dounby Head. 'They were at school together but Oliver was always a bit of a black sheep. When I was small he used to say he was my wicked uncle, but he's a sweetie really. I didn't see a lot of him when my dad was alive because they fell out over a business deal. My dad didn't like his business methods. But my mum had always got on well with him so sometimes I go to stay with him for holidays. My mum's a model did you know?' Tara said a little breathlessly. I glanced at her and I could sense her pride. I've always felt models to be about as socially relevant as giraffes, but I kept it to myself.

It had turned out to be a beautiful early summer day, slightly cold but with a soaring fresh sky and the moist grass was littered with colourful flowers and scents.

Oystercatchers screamed over the cliff tops. I digested the information she'd given me as I led the way to the old bench. The struts have been mostly broken off and the soil around the concrete blobs that the legs sit in has been eroded away so that one leg is precariously perched in air. The only way you can use the bench is to sit on the curved back and put your feet on what's left of the seat. Tara looked at it dubiously.

'It's all wet,' she complained.

'It's only dew. I'll wipe it.' I used the sleeve of my fleece.

'Wow! Neat view! There's a ship.'

'Fishing boat. And, see, further out, a yacht.'

'Xanthe's supposed to be buying a boat,' she told me. 'The other day she was on the phone to a man at a boat buying place.'

'She said she would,' I murmured, remembering her promise to take me out in it. I was sure I wouldn't be scared – or at least, I'd have to make a good show of pretending I wasn't.

She was looking at me. 'You haven't been up to the house since… you cut the grass.'

'Yeah. I thought phoning would be better.'

'How did you get on with my uncle?'

'All right,' I said grudgingly. I didn't know yet if I could trust her.

'I don't think you like him, do you?'

'He's a bit… domineering. How long have they…'

'He met her in London at a club. My mum was there too. Xanthe knew my mum years ago. I don't think they're, like, having sex. I don't know. He's supposed to be doing some deal… something about negative equity companies or something. That kind of bores me rigid. Anyway, my mum, you see, is in New York for the summer and I didn't want to go. I hate the city in the summer, especially New York, so I asked if I could come. I wanted to bring my friend, Suki, but uncle said there wouldn't be room. It's such a tiny place. I thought there would be loads of things to do but there isn't. I don't know how you bear it.'

'Yeah, well, I'll be going to University soon.'

'That's cool. I'll be doing that next year. My mum is trying to arrange something with a college in the States.'

'I'm thinking about Glasgow.'

She made a face. 'Euhhh! Is that not filled with drunks and junkies?'

'Where'd you hear that? It's Cultural Capital of Europe.'

But she wasn't listening. 'See over there?' Tara said. 'I'd like to go out there, beside the lighthouse. Can you, like, walk out?'

'Yeah, but you need to go up to the main road. It's too steep to walk on the cliff. You sure you can make it?' I asked, looking dubiously at her leather fashion boots.'

'Long as you don't go too fast.'

We set off, keeping to the high ground, with a panoramic sea view. You could almost see the headlands of the north coast, thirty miles away. Apart from a slight breeze, it was the perfect summer day. My head was full of songs and I wished I'd brought my Walkman. I felt suddenly mature, as if my life was starting now that I was ready to leave and go out into the world. I was looking forward to leaving. Tara seemed to me to be a kind of token of the outer world beyond Dounby, a world whose boundaries and frontiers were secure. I noted her interest in things I had long since lost curiosity about.

'So they used to collect the seaweed and like, dry it and sell it?' she asked. 'What a funny way to make money!'

Later, she pointed out some piles of stones. 'These used to be houses? People lived right here, on the cliff? But where did all the people go?'

I climbed onto the pile of mossy stones and looked down on her. 'God knows.'

She squinted up at me. 'Xanthe told me she met this friend of yours, J, in Glasgow years ago. It was when she was living there. There was a party for the art students and she went and like, this J was there because he was a... life model they call it? And they talked and he offered to pose for her.' Tara frowned. 'I don't know if he did but something must have happened – some trouble or something – and Xanthe didn't want to talk about it any more. Or it was maybe because Oliver came in...'

'When *did* Oliver come on the scene? When did they sort of get together?'

'Suppose it was quite recent. Because Xanthe was going out with another artist guy called Adrian at Christmas time. I know because my mum told me all about him. Bit of a scandal. The guy Adrian was still married, or just, anyway... Don't mention his name to Xanthe and don't say that I told you anything.'

'Of course not. Anyway, Mrs Pritchard doesn't talk about that kind of stuff to me. But she'd been coming here for years and last year and the year before that there was no one with her.'

'Maybe she just got bored with being up there all on her own?'

'Well... maybe...'

Tara turned away from me. 'Anyway, I hardly know her really; she's my mum's friend. We don't like, *talk*.'

I was getting confused. 'So Oliver is your mum's brother?'

'No, silly. Her brother-in-law. His surname is Harwood. Ours is Compton. That's my mum's surname. Oliver was high up in the City but there was some trouble and they moved out to Stevenage and Oliver went into property or something. To be honest, no one has a clue what he does but he's stinking rich. You never see him do anything, except smoke those beastly cigars. He's always on the phone though.'

'Not the sort of man I thought Mrs Pritchard would be interested in. I mean, he's a lot older and not exactly...'

She stopped and looked at me. 'You think she's fabulous don't you?'

After that, Tara clammed up. I think she resented me asking about Xanthe, and maybe she thought that I was more interested in Xanthe than in her. Which I was, to be honest.

We had reached the old road that leads to the automatic Lighthouse on Dounby Head. It is deeply potholed and there are even patches of weeds growing out of holes at the edge of the old tarmac. Dropping steeply down from us was the cliff that leads to the Witches' Craig and westwards to the Anvil Stane and Auld Darkney. We stood there for a while and I pointed the rocks out to her.

'What funny names,' she said. She walked over to the edge and looked down. 'So there's a beach there? You can't see anything.'

'Tide's in,' I said. 'You can hear the booming in the caves there though. Listen...'

'Oh yeah, you're right. So how do you get down there?'

I pointed out the track and how it led down between spurs of the cliff. 'It's not easy, especially if it's been raining. You have to hold on. In places, it's almost vertical.'

'Wouldn't get me going down there.'

'It's not too bad. The sand is beautiful there, you should see it. Fine and silvery and because it's so hemmed in by the cliffs, there's never any wind and it gets quite hot.'

But I could see that Tara could not imagine the potential of the secret beach.

'You know,' I said as we walked back by the main road, our shadows lengthening in front of us, 'when I first met you I thought you fancied Big J yourself.'

'Aw what? Euhhh!' was her first reaction. A few minutes later she said she'd thought he might be gay. It was a thought that had never even occurred to me.

'I just do not fancy him. He's not my type at all.'

'And am I your type?' I asked boldly.

She smirked. 'You could be. With the right clothes, the right haircut and the right kind of lighting behind you.'

'Fun-nee!'

5

'At the Coble Landing,' Alan spoke urgently. 'There's been some trouble. Come on, I'll tell you as we go. Some tossers from Scuggie Ness chased Rachel and Heather. There's talk of retaliation.'

I was back to being a teenager again. 'Where was this?'

'Up on the main road somewhere. A whole mob of them.' He spat dramatically on the ground. 'Townees!'

'Wonder if it's the same lot from last year? Bunch of hard nuts.'

There was a Council of War. Breeks was doing most of the talking, his shirt hanging out, standing on a drift log, with one or two others sitting on oil drums. Big J sat back against the shed door. He was keeping himself out of it mostly.

'We can't let them awa with it!' Field-Marshall J.J. 'Minger' Breeks, Chief of Staff, DSO and Bar, was saying. 'Trouble is how do we ken which anes it is that's caused the bother?'

Big J asked a question, aimed at me, not Breeks. 'Robbie – what happened last year?'

'Not a lot. Some skirmishing. It all petered out.'

'There's no way of knowing if it is the same lot?'

'Here's the lassies!'

A large mob of girls was moving towards us. Sixteen of them, almost every girl in Dounby. You could tell they were steaming.

Rachel Fyves was in the lead. 'Hear what happened?' she demanded. Rachel is tall, has masses of ginger hair and a pretty fearsome temper for just fifteen. Since second year, none of the boys ever messed with, or tried to mess with her. She's taller than most of us for a start.

'We was sexually harrassed,' Heather said importantly. 'By they English laddies at the caravan site.'

What were we going to do about it? they wanted to know.

'We'll get them,' Field-Marshall 'Minger' Breeks promised. 'We'll teach them...'

But none of the girls were paying him any attention. They were looking at Big J and Alan and me.

'If you don't do anything... we will!' the girls chorussed.

'Like, we're not going to stand for it,' Rachel said. 'We were doing nothing, just walking and all these laddies suddenly appeared behind a hedge. We thought we were going to be *raped*!'

'They kept chasing us for miles!'

One little kid at the back made some snidey remark and all hell let loose. Big J and me and Alan just sat and waited for everyone to calm down.

J jumped onto an oil drum and shouted for quiet. 'Okay. Okay. Right. Way I see it, the girls are upset. Quite right.'

'Bet we are! That's putting it mildly.'

'And those guys at the caravan park have a lot to answer for...'

Everyone was listening. Big J was calm. To me, then, he was like a military leader. He spoke with an air of authority. 'Thing is, only Rachel and Heather can point out which of them it was.'

'There was one laddie,' Heather said, 'greasy hair over his eyes, big... kind of...'

'...plukes...' put in Rachel.

'... yeah, pluky spots... and another one in a red tee-shirt... and a guy with dyed blond hair...'

'Dead short, like, shaved... He was pure dead ugly!'

'He was horrible!' And Heather started to cry.

Alan put his arm around her and loads of the girls did the same. Big J was still standing on the oil drum. 'So what I suggest...' he said quietly.

Everyone turned to listen.

'...we should do... is go over there and get the girls to point out the yobbos who did this and have a wee talk to them.'

'Yeah!' everybody shouted. 'Now you're talking!'

J's hand went up. 'But... and this is important... we're not a lynch mob. We go over there as a disciplined group. We have right on our side and just want justice.' He paused, looking at each of us. 'Yeah? Not revenge. That agreed?'

'Yeah,' everyone said, less enthusiastically than before.

'We want to avoid fighting if possible.'

The girls looked at each other but no one said anything.

'Because...' J's tone became honey-sweet, reasonable, almost pleading... 'because if that happens, we'll have a whole lot of trouble and we won't be able to enjoy the summer.' He sniffed, scratched the hair at the back of his neck. 'That agreed? It's important.'

'Uh-huh,' said a few people, me included.

'Another thing. I'm to do the talking when we get there. Okay?' He glanced around. 'Or I'm not going.' He came off the oil drum, looked around. There were no dissenting voices. 'Okay, let's head off.' He began to stroll away, hands bunched in his pockets. Like sheep, we followed, Alan and me first, then the rest. It must have looked impressive as we walked along the narrow strip of tarmac in front of the Seatown, across in front of the harbour and into the New Ground to the shingle path that begins to ascend to the cleft in the Lang Rock. A few people looked out at us, a small army we were of twenty or so, more joining from the village, some running down from the Braeheid. I didn't look back too much because I didn't want to lose my place just behind Big J, like his second lieutenant. Alan and I kept a bit ahead of the mass of girls and then behind them were a host of small fry and hangers on, most of the kids of the village. When we reached the handrail in the narrow pass between two big boulders, I glanced back and reckoned our numbers had swelled to about thirty. At the top, the village of Gardyne came into view, boats entering its harbour. It was bigger than Dounby, less precipitous and it had a primary school. On the level green slope above were the white cubes of the Scuggie Ness Caravan Park.

Biy J held up a hand and half-turned to me. 'Robbie, make sure nobody has any weapons of any kind, or anything that looks like a weapon.'

'Okay.'

'Will you do that? Make sure. Then catch up with us.'

I waited at the top of the rock. Heather and Rachel, still full of indignation were close behind.

'Why are you stopping, Robbie?' Heather asked.

'J wants me to see none of the wee eejits has any weapons.'

Rachel snorted. 'It's not weapons we need to sort them out. They'll get a piece of my mind.'

I counted thirty-seven, including some eight-year-olds who would not be persuaded, or bullied into going away.

'Get lost!'

'You can't stop us. We just want to see...'

I had to scramble to catch up with Big J. Breeks and Rob were up at the front.

'Rob. Thought you were studying?'

'Couldn't miss this. Ed and Stuart will be pissin themselves they've missed it.'

'A braw scrap that's just what we need, man,' Breeks went. He was jumping up and down in glee as if he was going to shite himself. 'Sort they emmits oot.'

'There's to be nae fightin,' I reminded him. 'That's what Big J said. It was all agreed.'

Breeks grinned. 'Aye, but they might start something... I'm hopin.'

There's a wide earth path that climbs above the beach onto the hillside above Gardyne. It leads to the clifftops and crosses the road and joins a tarmac track into the caravan park. Big J was leading the crowd up the slope.

'This is clever,' Alan said, 'nobody in Gardyne will notice us. Won't give the game away.'

'You're not wanting a fight too, are you?'

He grinned. 'Course no. You know how much I like Townees. It's a perfect end to the exams.'

'I'm not scrapping. Well, I don't think we should. There might only be a few of them. There are nearly forty of us. It wouldn't be fair.'

We hadn't seen any of the caravanners and we didn't think they could have seen us but there was an angry shout from somewhere in the village and we saw a youth in a white tee-shirt outside the bus shelter gesticulating at us.

'We've been spotted,' Alan said. 'Look along there!'

Coming towards us from the caravan park into the grass field was a large mob of youths, brandishing sticks and cricket bats.

'This is daft!' I said. 'There's at least twenty of them. And they're mostly bigger than us. We've only got a dozen – not counting the girls and the small fry.'

'And no weapons,' Alan said grimly.

The piece of the meadow between the two groups diminished till we were almost eyeball to eyeball.

'I'd better go back and get help!' Breeks whispered to me. I turned to see him scarpering. I was amazed – but there was no time to think of that.

'Naff off!' the caravan park youths shouted. 'This is our territory. You're not welcome here.'

'We're not here for a scrap,' Big J explained.

'What you doing here then?'

Big J held his arms out. 'Sit down lads,' he said to us. He looked over his left then his right shoulder. 'Just sit. Nobody say or do anything. I'm in charge.' Before we could do anything, he had sauntered forward within hitting distance of the other group. 'I'm the leader,' he said. 'Who's yours?'

'Me! I am,' said a weedy guy in a Newcastle United football shirt.

'Are you buggery! I'm the oldest,' said a tall, spotty youth in a red tee-shirt. You could tell they were both from Northern England.

'That's him!' cried Heather. 'One of them that's chased us!'

Big J held up a hand to silence her. 'I'm Big J,' he said firmly. 'What's your name?' he asked the guy in the football strip.

'I'm Nadger,' he said loudly, 'and this other ponce is me young bruv, Kevin. But I'm the man.' He was maybe sixteen, looked older, his hair was quite long.

'Okay, Nadge, let's do the leaders' thing and talk,' Big J said. 'Because we don't want to fight. We're only here to uphold the honour of our women.' The old-fashioned chivalrous language tickled us. I found myself smiling. 'Two of our women claim they were accosted by some of your people. Accosted and chased. I want to know if this is the truth.' We liked the word 'women'. I felt Heather beside me preen herself a bit at that.

'Oh, ye do?' Nadger said, looking over Big J at us. 'Well, we don't fight girls.'

'We don't fight anybody,' Big J countered. 'All we want is an explanation.'

'Yeah?' Nadger grinned. 'Yeah?' The guys behind him were spoiling for a fight. I reckoned maybe I could sort the little weed called Kevin but I didn't fancy Nadger at all. He had a strong build although most of it was podge. Some of the other guys looked handy though.

'I've had enough of this!' Rachel snorted. She pushed through to the front. 'You chased us and we was frightened.'

'Aye, we don't even know you!' Heather added.

'They've got a point, Nadge,' J said.

Nadger stood looking surly, face reddening. 'We don't fight girls,' he repeated.

There were warlike shouts from the youths behind him. I heard Rob shout something back. Rachel was angry, waving her fists about. It looked like world war three was about to erupt. Then J deflated the tension. He put his arm around Nadger's shoulder and led him away from his group. I was amazed, we all were.

'Nadger and I will need a few minutes to sort this out,' he declared over his shoulder. 'Sort out a compromise acceptable to both sides.'

Nadger nodded solemnly. I could see that Big J had won him over.

'So nobody do nothing till we get back,' J finished, 'or you'll have me to answer to. Me and Nadger.' This last was just a sop to Nadger's pride. It was obvious J was in total command of the situation. There must have been more than fifty of us up there all ready to fight to the death and J goes and puts his arm around the guy's shoulder and next thing we're all sitting down on the grass docile as sheep. Some of the girls are even casting lamb's eyes over at the youths from the caravan park mob. Discipline is breaking down all around and J and the youth Nadger are strolling off together to a sort of grassy mound about fifty yards away. It's like the battle of Bannockburn except Willie Wallace has suddenly decided to join the English.

So we all have a fag break, and I tell everybody about Breeks sneaking off to get help.

'Cowardly little shite,' is Alan's opinion. 'After all that hot air he was spouting earlier.'

And of course, none of the girls have a good word to say about him anyway. Then Big J and Nadger are coming back beaming all over their faces like they've just heard a great joke. And J says nothing at first, letting Nadger do the talking. He's not good at it but it's clear there's not going to be any scrap after all. I'm secretly pleased of course.

'We're sorry for chasing the girls,' he's saying. 'They started to run and we just followed.'

'Yeah,' Big J said. 'Seems they just wanted to invite you to the beach party.'

'Party!' Everyone was buzzing. 'What party?'

'On the secret beach, tomorrow afternoon,' J said. 'Yeah. There's going to be a barbecue and loads of good things to eat and drink and... smoke.'

'Dead brill!' everyone was going. 'Magic!'

And that's how peace broke out there on the hill above Gardyne. We all trooped back home elated that we had done something, that honour had been satisfied and looking forward to the party. Big J was the hero of the hour. It was a great triumph. I fell into step with him on the shingle beach.

'So what did you say to him?' I asked.

'Robbie, I can trust you to keep a secret?'

'Of course, no bother.'

'Nadge and I are mates,' he said. 'I met him days ago. I knew they didn't want to fight. But the party was my idea. It's maybe just what we all need to kick off the school holidays.'

'Yeah!'

'By the way, how did it go with Tara?'

I looked at him in surprise. 'How did you know...?'

He grinned. 'Oliver's away to London. Back on Saturday. Did Tara not tell you?'

'So you were up to see Mrs P— Xanthe?'

He beamed. 'Happened by chance. I was on my bike. Anyway, look. This party on the beach – there'll be hundreds there. Lots of people from Scuggie Ness, Gardyne and even Redstanes.'

'If we get the word around.'

'Don't worry, we will. Robbie, what do you think? I was going to ask Xanthe to come, or at least, I was going to bring her down.'

'That'd really make a statement!'

'No, but what I mean is... if you could bring Tara down. So nobody would think it odd, her just turning up like, with me, I mean.'

'Well, yeah, but what would she... Mrs... Xanthe think about it?'

'She's often talked about the beach. You took her a walk there one summer, didn't you?'

'I did.' Painful to remember my ridiculous and unrequited devotions of that time. It was the motive behind my secret months of physical exercise with the muscle-building flex-bar which I had sent away for. Anxiously I had peered in the mirror for signs of facial hair. To my chagrin, I hadn't even a faint excuse for shaving until just before my sixteenth birthday, although I remained remarkably free of plukes.

'I'll ask her tonight,' he said. 'I hear it's a great beach.'

'Yeah but it's too far away. People find it easier to go to Scuggie Ness, better road there. Access, car parks and that.'

'Yeah? Fancy taking a look now, Robbie? How long would it take us?'

'Half an hour maybe, if we go on your bike.'

'Let's do it.'

I have very early memories of Anvil Sands, from the first summer we came to Dounby. I haven't ever been back since that summer although I've made trips back to Dounby. The place had always had a mystique – a bad reputation – and I was banned from it as soon as my parents heard the rumours and that made it even more desirable. Apparently, a tourist was strangled there years ago and all kinds of weird goings-on happened, like nude bathing – skinny-dipping – and... well, anyway, since it's two miles along the coast on the other side of Dounby Head none of us bothered much with it. It's difficult to get down to, virtually inaccessible and although a lot of tourist coaches drive out on the narrow road to Dounby Head Light and take pictures of the sunset behind Auld Darkney or the Anvil Stane, few imagine there is a glorious beach there. Some people hire a powerboat from Redstanes Caravan Park. Then you can get in from the west by rounding the mighty buttress of Auld Darkney and the treacherous outcrops which have fallen from the Anvil Stane itself, and beach her in front of the caves of the Witches' Craig but the only way to get down to it on foot is by an almost vertical track from the cliffs, starting halfway along the road. The track is often so eroded in dry weather that you have to climb down a step at a time with the only handholds being the woody stems of gorse or clumps of ragwort. In wet weather, of course, it is impossible. At one point, the track reaches a rocky overhang, some forty feet above the water and you climb down from there on huge basalt blocks to the wedge of silver sand. The small beach is unexpected, tropical, exotic, and the sand is deep and luxurious, although barely forty feet at its widest, and curves up at each end. There is a stream, running out below the cliff and when the tide comes in, this swells and gradually isolates the high wedge of sand, then it is all overrun when the tide is fully in flood. The tides here are surly and dozens of folk over the course of history have drowned, caught unawares by the flood that has a dangerous undertow that can pull someone beyond reach in seconds. The unpredictability of the tide is related to the hidden reefs and deep rock fissures just below the surface. Best of all, once down on the beach, you are invisible from above, which is why I believe the tales of 'hanky-panky' as the oldies call it. We used to cycle up the main Duncairn–Redstanes road, along for a mile and a half, then down towards the Light, hide our bikes in a clump of bushes and race each other down to the beach. Getting back up was easier than getting down, even if you were stoned out of your nut. In the summer, the sun found its way to the sands about ten, shifted from one end of the beach to another and disappeared altogether about three-thirty so the best time to go was early. You never knew who would be there, although sometimes we went in huge groups, other times, it was just a small group of us, but mostly, nobody bothered and it was empty.

By the time Big J and I parked the bike at the top of the cliff and made the perilous descent down, where stones had dislodged themselves, where the turf and topsoil had been scoured by the wind and rain into a red mud-slick, the sun was dipping behind the Anvil Stane. Shadows were lengthening and only the wet edge of sand was in sunlight. The water fretting in the cove under the Anvil Stane was a luminous green you could see through to the sandy bottom.

I jumped down onto the sand and took off my trainers and socks. The sand was cool, dampish even. We were too late.

'The secret beach,' Big J said, taking out a cigarette. 'Certainly secluded. Looks as if it might get quite sheltered here.'

'It does. Gets hot,' I told him. 'I've been swimming here. Cold but bearable, not for long of course. In, out.'

'Nobody would bother you here,' he mused. 'Could go skinny-dipping. Sunbathe in the nude. I think I'll be coming here more often.'

I showed him the easy way up, which involved a steep scramble up some gigantic rocks to bring us out nearer to where he had propped the bike.

'Yeah,' he mused. 'Oliver's away till Saturday. I'm meeting her in Duncairn tomorrow. 'I wonder if she'd manage the climb here?'

'She did before.'

There was a long silence, and then he coughed and spat. 'You don't think she and Oliver...? I mean, have you heard anything from Tara about... their relationship, sort of thing?' To my amazement, he was blushing, or at least that's what it looked like.

'She says they're friends, that they're not having sex.'

He brightened. 'That's what she said?'

'She should know.'

'Great news.' He seemed profoundly affected. 'I had feared he was going to ask her to marry him. Thought maybe he was off to London to get the ring.'

Rather unkindly, I had laughed.

6

I awoke early the next day to the raucous squabbling of
seagulls. Through the thin bedroom wall I could hear
regular snoring and an occasional juddering old man's fart.
I pulled on my sweatshirt and combats and padded down
the creaky stairs to the kitchen. It was too early to eat
anything. I had a sip of orange juice from a carton in the
fridge but it was disgustingly thick and concentrated, the
cheapest kind, pure chemical, so I had to make do with
milk. I fastened my trainers and went outside and down the
hill. Nobody was up; it was way too early to call for Alan.
I sat a while in the earliest sunbeams of the day on the wet
bench among dew-silvered bushes in the allotments above
the Seatown, and then I went down the trodden clay track
to the lane of little houses. The lanes have religious names:
Strait Path, Exaltation Way, and Upper Green. One of the
little houses has a painted board on its wall:

Gospel Meetings...

If the Lord willeth, so the word of God be preached in this
room on Lord's Day at 6pm. You are welcome to do his
bidding.

Beside the matt black door to this house, fastened at an
angle into the concrete, was an enormous anchor. It
almost blocked the lane. Somebody had painted it black

over the rust and all. A kind of religious symbol maybe. I came out on the narrow strip of concrete that ran along the seawall. Beyond the end of this, Breeks and his stepmother, Ada, lived up a clay path overgrown on both sides. The wall of their house was built in close to the red sandstone so that it looked as if grass and weeds were sprouting from their corrugated iron roof. I bent down to peer into the windows. There were no sounds of life. A cardboard box at the door contained five empty wine bottles – Chateau de Plonko – a heap of beer cans of the cheapest, no-label brand. I disturbed a cat, a mangy black and white specimen, poking tentatively under a rotting, slimy creel.

I made a low whistle under my breath and clicked my fingers. It looked warily at me for a few moments then retreated. I kicked at a stone then went back down to the seawall. Some starched washing creaked on lines wound between wooden posts. The tide was distant, less than a rumour. I saw Breeks among the rocks. He was hunkered down, gathering whulks. He glanced up at me, squinting under the palm of his hand.

'You're up early Robbie!'

'Getting whulks?'

'Aye. A wee baggie for McAdams. Give's a hand.'

'That's a lot ye've got!'

Breeks grinned widely. 'Aw naw, I had this lot yesterday. Tie them in the bag see so they keep fresh. McAdam's disna open till the afternoon. Sixteen pee a pund, man. I've got ten, maybe fifteen pund a'ready.'

'That's not a lot. God, Breeks! I gave up pulling whulks when I was about eight.'

'Aye, well,' he sniffed. 'It's a'right if ye work steady at it. Ye need to get the low tide. Most mornins I'm out here.'

'Goin to the beach party, Breeks?'

He looked at me as if I was mad. 'Course, man. Course ah'm goin. I mean how no?' He poked his penknife blade into a slobbery whulk and swallowed it, then burped. 'I'm hopin to sell a quarter ounce maybe to some of the lads at the caravan park.'

'Oh, the lads you didn't want to fight?'

Breeks laughed. 'Aye, right.'

'Ye've no shame?'

'How should I? A deal's a deal. What do I care if some guys had a feel o Rachel Fyve's tits? I mean man, you canna blame them. It wasn't possible that I could start to fight with Nadger and his guys after I'd been talking to them about business. Know what I mean? I'm a business man, like.' He tossed two handfuls of whulks into the jute sack and tentatively tested its weight. 'I reckon that's me up tae the twenty pund.'

'So that was why you scarpered?'

'Course, man. How else? I'm no feared of a scrap but business comes first. Fancy a cup a tea?'

We walked across the shingle. The sun was making the roofs and walls of Dounby look like a fairy village, almost Mediterranean. I could smell the drying kelp. The screech of seagulls, the almost nonexistent lap of the water far out on rocks.

'Business is the only way out of here,' Breeks was saying. 'I was thinkin o going to the Merchant Navy like, but I don't have the two O-levels. And they found out about my time in the borstal.'

'So what are you doing now, apart from a little dealin?'

Breeks grinned. 'Deals, man. D'ye think...?' he studied my face for a moment. 'I've been thinking about a great deal, man, a real cracker... but I'd need to have some of the lassies under my power.'

'Breeks – dream on!'

'Naw man, just think... if I could have power over Rachel and some of them... lots of guys'd pay big money to just chat to them, like, or anything more and we could make loads of bunce, man. Imagine? There's big profits in the sex trade, bigger than sellin dope because you get aulder guys wi big pay packets, ken aff the rigs or that...'

'Breeks!'

'What?'

'I'd stick to the whulks if I were you.'

'Naw, but, maybe the girls'd go for it... braw money...'

'Give it up, man!'

I had been in Breeks' place once before. When we were wee before he'd been sent away. I never knew him at school. He'd been sent to a special school in Duncairn. A blue van with iron grilles on the window used to call for him on a Monday and didn't bring him back till Friday night. Where he lived was little more than a shack. He was rather proud of his 'pad' as he called it. Since there was only one bedroom where his stepmother slept up to eighteen hours of every day, Breeks had a mattress on the floor in the other room. He had nailed a rope across a corner of the room and hung a striped curtain over it. Inside was a tangled heap of jeans and underpants and tee-shirts. At the other side of the room was a sink under the window and a table cluttered with a half-used milk bottle, cereal packets and ashtrays brimming with cigarette stubs.

'Yer mum away?' I asked as we entered.

'Naw,' he said cagily, 'she's in, and that.' He looked worried. 'Asleep like. I'll get the kettle on.'

Breeks lifted the lid off a plastic bucket and dipped a battered, blackened aluminium kettle into it.

'What's wrong with the tap?'

'Aw, it's... ye ken... Dinna worry.'

I peered at the bucket. 'Disna look very hygenic, man. There's beetles and all sorts in there.'

'Fresh water, man!' he insisted. 'S'all right.'

There was a roar nearby.

'What the hell's that?'

'S'all right, s'all right. Just my maw bawlin in her sleep maybe.'

'WURREH!'

'Is she all right?'

Breeks looked up from wiping two mugs with a filthy cloth. 'Wha cares? Cos I dinna.'

The door was flung open and Ada stood in the doorway in a crumpled, stained nightshirt. Her grey hair was all over the place and the nightshirt barely covered her thighs. Loose folds of skin hung down at the back of her knees.

'Wha's that?' she roared. 'Wha have ye brung wi ye – ye wee bugger?' She wiped her eyes and roared: 'Wha is it?'

'None o your business ye auld hoor!' Breeks muttered.

'It's me, Mrs – Robbie Strachan,' I said.

'Well ye can get oot o it, Robbie Strachan!'

'He's just haein a cup of tea, mither!'

'Naw, he's no. And you can piss off oot o it an a'! Get!'

I left him to it. As I got back onto the path I heard glass breaking in the shack. I set off along the shingle and walked to the Maiden Stane then I cut home for breakfast. It was going to be a fine day.

In our part of the world, the 'hinmaist pairt' according to Hecky, you don't expect much in the way of a summer. It was always an anxious time if the sun rose early and the sky seemed blue. Old men with nothing better to do would sit at the harbour and spit and scan the sky and summon by sheer willpower the clouds and rain. Old women would lean out of their doors dubiously and prognosticate pessimistic forecasts. 'It's comin, aye, mark my words, son... it's comin. There'll be a reckoning.' All the TV weathermen too seemed to be antagonistic. It was like we didn't *deserve* a sunny day, not a full day and if it did occur, then you could be sure tomorrow would be stormy right enough.

Big J was standing alone on the beach, wearing a colourful pair of Bermuda shorts that showed off his strong legs. With his dark tan and dark hair he might have been a South Seas islander or an Aztec. He had constructed a rough barbecue range protected by rocks and had a fire going inside it.

He beamed. 'Robbie! Good timing man. Help me get the fire going.'

'Okay, J, but... where's the grub?'

He grinned at my lack of faith. 'It'll get here. Plenty time for that.' He pointed at a heap of wood over by the rocks. 'Start off with those. And here's firelighters.' He tossed over the packet. 'Got matches?'

'Uh-huh.'

'Sorted.' He put his arm on my shoulder and grinned broadly. 'She's coming down,' he said exultantly. 'At three-thirty. I've to meet her at the top of the cliff.'

'Yeah?' I had mixed feelings about it. 'How did it go at Duncairn yesterday?'

'Absolutely... ecstatic. She's wonderful!'

'I'm pleased for you.' He saw my glum expression and laughed. 'She's bringing Tara you know. Or at least, I asked her to.'

'Tara told me she couldn't come.'

'Well, we'll see.' He pointed to two cardboard boxes that he must have carried down by himself. 'I'll be fixing myself a drink.' He grinned. 'You'll get one when you get the job done.'

'And what will you be doing?'

Big J just laughed and did a little barefoot dance on the sand.

I began to lug the logs and driftwood over to the barbecue site. I heard voices from above and saw about a dozen people clambering down the rocks onto the beach. I soon got a good fire going and became absorbed in the task.

'Robbie!' I heard Big J shout, and then he beckoned.

I sauntered over. There were several girls. I didn't know any of the people. As fast as J told me their names, I forgot them. There were more people coming down from the cliffs, some carrying boxes and crates of drink. One of them kicked off his shoes and came running over. He had his guitar in its case slung around his neck.

'Oh, man! Look at this place!' Like Baywatch!' He scooped up a handful of sand and let it sift through his fingers. 'Tropeecal maaan! *Arriba arriba, Ow! Ow!*'

By now there were scores of people on the beach, all the hippies from miles around, mostly Big J's age or older. They dispersed into little groups on the sand, or clustered around the barbecue.

'Robbie! Drag over more wood for the fire,' Big J called. 'By the way,' he said, when I got over to where he was standing, 'this is Shona.' He grinned and kissed her hand. 'Shona's from Edinburgh. She's at the Uni. Isn't that where you're going, Robbie?'

I looked at her glumly. 'I'm not sure yet.'

She was a tall redhead in a yellow halter-top, whose teeth were fixed in a metal brace visible when she smiled. 'Oh yes,' she chirruped. 'What're you going to do?'

'Sorry?'

She looked cross. 'Study. What are you going to study?'

'Ehm... I don't know really, maybe science.'

'Science?' She made it sound like a disease. 'But which?'

'Pardon?'

'Oh, never mind!' she snorted and turned back to her friends. End of conversation. I couldn't think of anything to say to get her interest. I made up for the snub by becoming very active with the wood and the fire. I had no idea why Rob and Ed and Stu hadn't shown up.

J was sitting on an old deckchair beside a cardboard crate of beer cans. He handed me a beer.

'Tony's on his way with the food,' he said. 'We'll need to get a gang together to help him down with the stuff.' He glanced at his wristwatch and winked. 'And you and I need to be ready to move in about twenty minutes.'

'Who's Tony?'

He stretched his arms above his head. 'Ah, you wouldn't know him. Works in a meat wholesaler in Duncairn. He's arranged all the food. For free, like.'

It was no surprise to me that after only a few months in Dounby, Big J had built up connections and had mates everywhere.

'Hardly anybody here from Dounby,' I observed. 'Or the Scuggie Ness lot.'

'Well you know, parties aren't really their thing. They're a bit young yet, you know. Mind, I thought Ed and Rob and that lot would make it.'

'So where are these lot from then?'

J grinned. 'Couple of phone calls to mates in Redstanes and the Halls of Residence at Duncairn. They're mostly students. One or two, like Bill and that lad over there, Herbie, work at Redstanes caravan park.'

As he was speaking, I saw Rob and Ed and Stu and Alan with Yvie and Lila and loads of others picking their way down the cliffs.

'Great! Here they come!'

J looked round and began to test his upper teeth with his thumbnail. Then he slugged his beer. 'Wonder what they'll think about it?' he said reflectively. 'I mean, me and Mrs P?'

'Who cares?' I said vehemently. 'It's no one's business but yours and Mrs... Xanthe's.' Of course, I deeply envied him then but maybe stronger already by that time was my comradeship with him. That he had singled me out as worthy of his companionship and important enough to be his confessor gave me powerfully mixed emotions.

Somebody had put a reggae tape into a ghetto blaster. Everyone began shaking to it, spilling tight little shadows on the early afternoon sand. The guitar man was trying to chord along with it, every now and then letting out a yelp: *Arriba! Arriba!* I squatted on the crates of beer cans, enjoying the play of light across my face from the reflections of the aluminium and the cold spray of lager on my throat.

'What did you feel when your dad died?' Big J suddenly asked. He saw my surprise and waved his can in a tight circle. 'No, man, I just want to know what it felt like. How old were you again?'

'I was ten,' I told him. 'I don't remember much about it. I suppose I blanked a lot of it. He was ill for quite a long time. I suppose at that age, it's hard to work out what's happening.'

'I suppose so,' he said gloomily. 'I never knew my dad. Or my mother. I was brought up in an Orphanage in Glasgow.'

'I didn't know that.'

'It's a long time since I told anybody. Like you, I suppose I blanked a lot of it. Before I went to the Orphanage, I was passed around a lot of distant relations, most were very old. I remember living in Hull for a while then London. Then the Orphanage.'

'What was it like?'

'Not good. At first, I didn't mind too much. I thought it was quite a friendly place. It was a while before I realised anything was wrong.'

'What was wrong?'

'Well... I made friends – most just a year or two older than me – who kept running away and getting brought back and later I found out the man who was running the place had friends who were... abusing the kids in the place. It was a paedophile network. I had no intention of putting up with it so I skedaddled. At that age – I was thirteen – it's quite easy to lose yourself. I looked older than I was.'

'Why didn't you report the man?'

'Be serious, Robbie!' he smiled faintly. 'Who's going to believe the word of a thirteen-year-old? I certainly wasn't an angel either.'

'Where did you go then?'

'I reckoned I'd have a better chance in the city so I got the night bus to London and joined up with a bunch of squatters in Clapham. They became my family for a couple of years, and then I went abroad with the Merchant Navy. That's when I got my real education. There was an A.S. I shared a cabin with for nearly a year who lent me his books and taught me about poetry and philosophy.'

'So who was the woman that came here with you? People thought she was your aunt.'

'No, no. Ellen was a social worker I used to know. She'd been kicked out because of her alcohol problems. I was helping her to stay dry. A friend of hers got a council house swap. But she's moved back to Glasgow.' He smiled thinly. 'Contrary to rumours she's under the garden shed.'

'I never believed that.'

'I'm glad. Did I tell you I have poetry published?'

'I think you told me you wrote poems.'

He nodded solemnly. 'In London, I used to go along to writers' workshops and poetry readings. It was a good way of getting to meet nice people. Didn't get paid for the poems though. This was in the late seventies. Hey!' he jumped to his feet. 'It was about time you passed us a joint.' He sat down and inhaled once, then again. 'This is brilliant, here on this beach, just hanging out.'

'Do you really like Xanthe?'

He laughed as he passed me the joint. 'Note of jealousy there, mate?'

I ignored that. After a few moments, I tried again. 'You told me you met her in Glasgow?'

'Did I tell you that?'

'You said you'd been a life model at the Art College.'

'I knew of her,' he said. He stood up. 'Fire needs stoking. Here comes the food.'

I looked up and saw somebody at the top of the cliffs waving.

* * *

The beach party was the only topic of conversation for weeks afterwards. The sudden appearance of Mrs Pritchard on the arm of Big J had given the gossips something to get their teeth into. As for me, the non-appearance of Tara – as I had anticipated – had thrown me into despair. No one knew of course and no one interested anyway in anything except the hot gossip of the moment.

'She's a terrible flirt,' Yvie complained. 'Even when she was with Big J, you could see her eyeing up all the other blokes.'

'And those shorts left nothing to the imagination!' Rachel Fyves said. 'She's in her forties!'

'Na, she's no. She's only about thirty,' I snarled. 'Get a life!'

'You know what?' Lila sneered, 'you're getting like Big J's wee bum-chum these days.' They turned away from me. 'You've spent too much time with her!'

'Maybe she's into threesomes,' Yvie suggested evilly.

'Fun-nee!'

But it was true. Mrs Pritchard and J seemed natural together and somehow I was part of it, although how I couldn't exactly explain. It was a sort of conspiracy and the deeper I got into it, the further I seemed to be taken from Tara or my friends. I seemed to be seeing less of Alan too. He was always in Duncairn. Never at home.

'It's the school play,' he told me. 'I'm really into it. Doing the scene painting and that. There's some gorgeous lassies in the cast too.' That puzzled me a bit, didn't really sound like Alan – another mystery.

Rob and the Vampire Invaders were getting gigs in hotels in Redstanes and Ed's dad's van was always on its way to, or back from, some gig somewhere.

'We're getting paid now,' he'd told me proudly at the party. 'Got fifty quid coming. Tenner each.'

Josh showed his missing tooth. 'Play all night for a tenner, man. You should see the women that comes to the gigs, man!'

The only one missing out was me, it seemed. Tara would phone me and chat for hours till my stepfather practically broke my door in, then she wouldn't call for days when she promised she would. I couldn't make it out. I was tearing my hair out. Why couldn't she be straight with me?

'Told you,' J said brightly. 'She's fifteen. It's a difficult age.'

'Look,' I snapped. 'For the last time, she's sixteen. In fact, in the winter, she'll be seventeen!'

'Have it your own way, man,' he grinned. He turned at the door. 'But have it, man. Is my advice.'

'Hey, what do you mean by that?' I shouted but he was gone. I heard the front door slam.

My mother came up the stairs with a cup of tea. 'Your friend was in a hurry!'

'That's just his way.'

'Is he in your class?'

'No, no.'

'I was going to say. He seems older. I presume you haven't heard from your girlfriend?'

'No, ma, I haven't. Why?'

'Just wondered why you had such a long face.'

'Well; now you know. Thanks for the tea.'

After she'd retreated downstairs of course, I started regretting being short with her. I was so used to being defensive. In Dounby you have to have a story ready. I was quite sure she'd have heard all about Big J and the American lady by now anyway from someone – everyone – at the Church Ladies. They met on Monday nights at the Hall of the Church of the Second Chance. She hadn't said anything but I could tell from the set of her shoulders at the kitchen sink when she was peeling potatoes that she knew something. It wasn't a subject I wanted to have discussed in the house so I went out to clear my head, away from the village, up by the main road to the junction then along towards Redstanes.

* * *

Tara finally lowered herself to call on the Wednesday. I was down in the Beach Café, sitting on my own, reading a book, the dregs of a coffee in front of me. I wasn't really reading the book, I was ruminating in an idle fragmented way about the coming summer and how it was not working out as I had imagined. The little group whom I had spent so much time with over the last couple of years seemed to have gone their separate ways and when we came upon each other we seemed to have nothing to say or we fought about nothing at all. It was as if Dounby had suddenly got too small for us. Or as if we had suddenly tired of each other's company. Each of us went around the place imagining that everyone else was conspiring against us, or saying poisonous things about us to the others. There was no cohesion any more. I had begun to suspect that this was a mutually acquired method of softening the inevitable wrench when we all left Dounby because it would happen and it would be a wrench and there would come a day when we would walk down the Braeheid and see no one who knew us. It would be almost painful to be in the place and see no one you were really close to. The place was busy of course because the tourists were flooding the coastal villages. You could always see Yvie or Lila in the Shoprite if you wanted but they had acquired a veneer of indifference, a waspish, unpleasant edge to everything they said. I had begun to wonder if this sense of us as a 'set' was only in my mind. If the others had ever felt it at all. Of course, the skeleton crew was still visible: Shopsoiled Susan and Village Bobby – more often on display at the pier these days with his shiny buttons – to impress the tourists. And Social Worker was usually in his place on the bench outside the Church Hall that gave him a panoramic view of the whole village. And Hecky came and went in the daylight and at night-time too, drunk and sober, like a ghost. You rarely saw him on his doorstep these days. He was getting more work on the boats. Billy Murrell had gone for the summer to work the boats round on the west coast. 'Oot after the mackerels,' someone had said. Sandy Stokes was still about though. Still leaning on his counter, welcoming the tourists with his phony American bonhomie and his sour-smelling tee-shirts, 'What'll it be, darlin?' Heather and Rob Lowdy were away on holiday with their parents. I was beginning to miss her exuberance. At least she seemed to like me for myself.

'You had a phone call,' mum said, when I slouched in the back door. 'That Tara girl.' She smiled. 'The call you were waiting on, I think?'

'Oh yes,' I murmured, stone-faced. 'Tara.'

'Nice lassie. Here for the summer just. Staying with that American lady.'

'Did she say she'd ring back? Or was I to ring her?'

Mum gave me one of her funny looks. 'You should ring her. Take the initiative, Robert! Instead of sulking about.'

'I'll do that. Where's John?'

'Overtime. Won't be back till eightish.'

'Good for him.'

'Tea'll be ready in ten minutes.'

'I'm not hungry.'

'Ten minutes!' she called after me as I went up the stairs.

* * *

I found myself up early next morning. I was getting up earlier than I ever had when I was supposed to be getting up early for school. It was a whiteout, thick haar covering everything. I couldn't see the windows of the house next door.

My stepfather was at work and my mother had gone out. I took a piece of toast, put on my wellies and my parka and went out into it. It was an incredible phenomenon. I've seen it like this and then up on the main road, it's bright and sunny. I felt like walking, like being invisible. I saw occasional ghostly shapes and muffled lights in windows but I set off along the cliff path. It wasn't cold. Words from some Leonard Cohen songs came into my head and I sang them doing the grating voice. It's amazing what you can remember. I liked their wistful melancholy. The lyrics of an international man, a world-traveller. I particularly liked 'Famous Blue Raincoat' from *Songs of Love and Hate* but they were all memorable, as good as Kristofferson. I hadn't mentioned my interest to the others, nor my interest in classical music either. I knew what they'd say. It wasn't 'with it'.

Occasionally the haar would open up a little to reveal the black vulture-like presence of shags preening themselves on rocks, necks arched, disputing with seagulls or silent and brooding like clergymen watching the tide. I came out onto the tarmac road that led to the Light and the farm, Dounby Home Farm which had been converted into two cottages, one of which was let out as a B & B, the other was let on long leases. In the summer it was a picturesque place, whitewashed walls, roses and honeysuckle overwhelming a dilapidated wooden trellis arch. The garden, behind drystane dykes, was mostly overgrown, with several stunted apple trees and bushy rowans. It hadn't been let for a year and that seemed odd to us because it was just the kind of place that would attract eccentrics, lettuce-eaters, bird-worshippers and hairy-toed female sandal-wearers. I began to see the ghost of the buildings and I heard a car engine. I turned around and looked for the narrow sheep track that led down to Anvil Sands. Then I saw the car. I knew straight off it was Mrs Pritchard's. There was no one inside it. There could only be one reason why it was here. She had come to walk on the beach, but was she alone – or with Big J?

I began to clamber down the track onto the cliff edge. Huge drifts of incoming haar trailed upwards. The grass was heavy with water. Here and there patches of light appeared, and faded. The path down the cliffs was slippery and difficult in wellies. I had to use my hands. Long before I got to the bottom I heard the murmur of voices and once a laugh. I was preparing a story in case I suddenly came on them when I realised I could see where they were. They were lying on a tartan rug in the sand at the water's edge near to the spur of the rock that trailed into the sea. I sat down behind a rock and watched. I could only see their lower halves but – it looked as if they were naked! I carefully went back the way I had come. When I reached the place where water flows out from the rock, I began to scramble up the cliff. I scraped my knees but I kept on going. I was terrified that they might have seen me or might be coming up after me. All I had seen was their legs and thighs, hers slim and white, his dark and hairy. I had been so close! Not for the first time, I envied him. I imagined how wonderful it would be to be him at that moment, loved by her! I felt the desolation of the thought that she preferred him to me niggling against the recollection that he had singled me out as his confidante. My feelings of desire for her, for all we had shared together, admittedly all on my side, unrequited, warred with my feelings of awe and admiration for Big J.

When I got back to the road, I realised that it would be safer to walk along the road to the main road junction and then down to Dounby than picking my way along the cliffs. Maybe I had a subconscious desire for them to see me, to know that I had been out in the area too. After all, anybody could have come across the car and followed the track down to the beach – and come upon them. Oliver, for instance. I began to think what it would be like if it was Tara and I on the sand instead of Big J and Mrs Pritchard but the idea just kept fading before I could get it pictured.

I didn't hear the car behind me until the horn blasted. I jumped out of the way. It was her. She wound down the window. There was no sign of Big J. She smiled out at me happily.

'Robert! What a pleasant surprise! I'd like to give you a lift.'

As I got into the car I found myself struck blank with visions of her wet nakedness and watched her face for signs of guilt. Strangely, I found that I was the one who was embarrassed.

'What a day!' she gushed, changing gear. I couldn't believe she wanted to talk about the weather and sat morosely staring out.

'Out for a walk were you?'

'Uh-huh.'

'A real pea-souper, isn't that what they say?'

'I saw you on the beach,' I said, feeling my guts wrenching. When she looked at me, I felt the sudden twitch of desire. 'By accident,' I added hastily. 'I had no idea you were there.'

She gave me a knowing look. 'Oh dear, you must have found it embarrassing. It was a spur of the moment thing. It's difficult at the moment, as I'm sure you'd understand. I hope we can rely on you to keep our little secret?'

I coughed. 'Oh yes, of course.'

We'd reached the road junction and Mrs Pritchard looked left and right before turning into the B8760, the Redstanes to Duncairn road. There were no vehicles in sight. 'It is difficult just now. With Oliver about, I mean.' She glanced conspiratorially at me and smiled and patted my knee.

'Oliver, yes?' I repeated. 'What does he actually do?'

She frowned. 'He claims to be an entrepreneur. Something to do with stocks and equities, whatever those are. You'd have to ask him.' She placed her hand on my knee. I could feel its warmth through my jeans. 'As far as Oliver is concerned,' she purred, 'he's my biggest mistake in recent times.'

'Tara thinks you are just friends.'

Mrs Pritchard shook her hair free and sniffed. 'Ah, Tara, bless her.' She indicated for the left turn to Dounby. 'Oliver has rather taken advantage of the situation. He makes assumptions which he is simply not free to make.'

This did not make sense to me at the time.

'Would you like to come in for coffee?' she asked. 'I think Tara will be there, unless Oliver has taken her to the riding school. And by the way would you please call me Xanthe, not that awful Mrs Pritchard. We know each other well enough I think.'

'Thank you.' My heart sank at the thought of Tara seeing me in my wellies and green jumper with the sleeves out and baggy cheapo supermarket jeans.

Mrs Pritchard – I simply could not get used to the idea of calling her Xanthe – parked the car on the hard standing and we went inside.

'First, Robert, there is something I'd like you to see, if you will.' She glanced at my footwear and the wet trail on the carpet. 'We'll go back out the front door,' she said, plucking my sleeve. We walked around the house to the dilapidated wooden shed that stood off by itself in a little dip. A former double garage, it had a much repaired felt-tiled roof and its double doors hung squint and snagged on the tufts of grass which had burst through the ancient concrete base. It was where the petrol mower lived. The padlock hung from a wooden bar but it was too rusted to use, so the place was open throughout the year. 'What do you think of this?' Mrs Pritchard asked proudly, drawing me inside. It smelt, as usual, of linseed oil and cobwebby dryness. I looked around. There was nothing much inside to steal; some ancient gardening implements and the two dilapidated bicycles whose tyres were soft and laced with splits which had been there ever since I can remember. A cable looped to the striplight screwed to the rafters. But most of the usual clutter had been piled in the far corner. A space had been cleared in front of the single window that was protected with chicken wire. Xanthe picked up a heavy steel implement that lay on a metal trestle table. 'This is a metal cutter,' she said. 'It slices through everything as if it was peanut butter. And look, I've had some metal things delivered.' Behind her stood a motley collection of sad metal objects, rusty bits of metal, all kinds of scrap, a flattened petrol can, most of a car door, a gas cylinder, half of a washing pole... it was tragic. She gazed on it all fondly. 'I can't wait to get started,' she said. 'You see, Roberto, what I do is cut bits of metal off and load them in the furnace. That's here.'

'Wow! A furnace. That's new.'

'I had it delivered from Duncairn yesterday. Isn't it sweet? So the metal bits go in here, I fire it up and then it gets poured out here into these moulds. The best thing is, I can use almost any type of metal. In fact, Robert, the more varied the mix, the more interesting the texture.

Then I use the oxy-acetylene torch to construct my pieces, welding them together.'

'It's a lot of work,' I commented.

'That's the best thing about it. Lots of good physical exercise, get rid of the tensions.' She undid her sleeve and rolled up her shirt and flexed her biceps. She had perfectly toned arms, bigger muscles than me. 'What do you think?'

'Lovely,' I muttered.

'Why thank you, kind sir!' She fastened her sleeve. 'I have to wear a leather apron and steel toecap boots and leather gloves of course, but it's exhilarating. It really is. I work up a great sweat. It's the perfect combination of physical and mental exercise.'

'So what are your pieces like?'

'Oh, I can show you some old pieces – just early efforts – in the house, but I'm working on new ideas for figurines. Human shapes. I suppose you'd, um... call it a cross between Classical and Cubist conceptions of the human form.'

'Right.'

'You're not that interested, are you? I can tell. Pity.'

'No really. It's great.'

'I was going to ask if you'd come up and help me with the smelting. I'd pay you of course.'

'I could, yeah.'

'Don't sound so enthusiastic! Beauties aren't they?' Xanthe was admiring the rusty old oxy-acetylene torch and cylinders on their little trolley. 'Of course, I still intend to do the usual metal casting as well, but the idea of welding plates is new to me. Allows for a more...' she paused, '... *industrial* appearance. Anyway, enough art! Let's go inside. Oliver will be wondering what we're doing out here!' she said with a wickedly wilful grin.

As she pulled the doors to, I savoured that. 'I'd be glad to help. Really, I would.'

'We'll see,' she said. Hiding my disappointment at this inconclusive remark, I meekly followed her into the house.

The kitchen got the afternoon sunlight and it splashed about like torchlight. The walls were orange, hung with strings of garlic and corn dollies and the cupboards and worktops had a mellow wood look. A coffee percolator gave off little wisps of steam. Oliver stood at the chopping board, slicing onions and peppers. He wore a plastic apron that read *The National Trust*... but I knew that I did not trust him. He half-turned. 'Hello, stranger. Like a cup of coffee? Tara's about... Tara!'

'I'm all right thanks.'

He slid the onion slivers into a pan on the hob and wiped down the chopping board. He sniffed. 'Please yourself, matey. Have a seat.' Then he selected some herbs and chopped them with the same knife in a fast and professional manner. 'Love cooking, I do,' he said. 'Relaxing. Forces you to concentrate so you forget your other troubles. Sit down, Bob.' Then he seemed to remember and added, 'Ah, I mean Robert.'

I sat and watched him. He found an Oxo cube and crumbled it into the pan. 'Of course, I'm not your actual chef-type. I stick to the familiar everyday kind of scran.'

'Smells nice.'

'Thanks. Sure you don't want a coffee?' he peered at me from his heavy eyebrows. 'Xanthe been showing you her forge?' He gave a short laugh. 'The forger's art, hey?'

Mrs Pritchard came in then. She placed two metal figurines on the table. 'These are the only two I have here,' she said. 'What do you think?'

Oliver snorted. 'Those rusty old things!'

I looked at him and then at them. 'But they're great!'

Xanthe leaned over and touched my cheek. 'Why thank you Roberto! You see – not everyone is a philistine like you,' she teased Oliver.

'I was only kidding!' Oliver complained.

The figurines were about two feet high, abstract male figures, long-limbed, almost skeletal and their heads were smaller than you would expect. The faces were blank except for a ridge where you'd expect the nose to be. It was like a beak. There was something vulnerable yet predatory about them.

'I do like them,' I said. 'How much do you sell them for?'

They laughed together and Oliver wiped his hands on his apron. 'Thinking of buying one? There's a waiting list you know.'

'Is there? I didn't know.'

'He's only teasing you. But generally my work is commissioned. Each piece goes for... well, depending on size, between two and three thousand.'

'Two and three thousand pounds?'

'No, dollars. That's less. Depends on size though.'

'How many do you make at one time?'

'Well... maybe two at a time, not more... each is meant to be unique. Of course, some have to get melted down if something goes wrong, you know, if there's something not perfect. Air bubbles... that sort of thing.'

'By the way Bob,' Oliver said pleasantly, 'you know that chap that has the motorbike, don't you. A tallish chap, little bit older than you maybe?'

I looked at Xanthe and I may have been imagining it but she seemed to freeze. 'Yeah, he's a friend of mine.'

'I don't like the look of him,' Oliver said. 'He's been hanging around. I hope he's not pestering Tara. I mean, she hasn't said anything but she's due to go back to her parents soon and I don't want any scruffy no-mark taking advantage of her, know what I mean?'

'Oliver! That's quite enough of that!' Xanthe said sharply.

'Tara hasn't said anything,' I said, catching her eye.

'Glad to hear it!' Oliver snorted. 'Now could you get those works of art off my table. I have my own work of art to create!'

7

The telescope was powerful enough to study the pattern of the waves, examine the shoreline faintly visible across some thirty miles of the sea to the north west, to count seals, dolphins, whales, even the mighty sea-unicorns which sported beyond the horizon, the occasional giant waltzing cod even. I could imagine Xanthe watching, at sunset, as the selkies changed into rocks, the naiads clustered amongst the seaweed, the sand porpoises emerged from their lair, seeing all the mythical sea creatures that dance when the last human eye is...

The door opened. 'It's marvellous to sit here and look through it,' she said smirking, handing me a hot mug of coffee. 'It's amazing what you can see. When you get a day clear of this goddamn fog.'

'It's very powerful,' I said meekly. 'It says it's times fifty magnification.'

Mrs Pritchard sat on the cushioned bay-window seat. 'Oh, Roberto, Roberto!' she sighed. 'You've no idea what a heaven this place is to me. Put the telescope down and come and sit by me.' She patted the seat cushion next to her. Humbly, I did her bidding. She had changed into casual clothes; a white silk blouse, lycra pedal pushers and loose leather sandals, and tied her hair with a white scrunchy which made her look Italian or Mexican and also rather girlish. I felt myself getting hot and my blood starting to throb. *Maybe...*

She leaned back. I could smell the exotic shampoo in her hair. 'The pleasure it is not to have to shop or jostle on the subway, to be able to spend all day about my art, or walk by the sea. With a good book or a bottle of wine or just counting the waves on the beach.' She lifted one leg up into her lap and massaged her calf. 'Not that you're ever entirely free...' she nodded at the door and smiled conspiratorially. 'Anyway, when I said I was coming here again, for the fourth year, they all went... "You're going where? On your own?" Of course, they didn't know about Oliver. That didn't happen till later. Anyway Serge – have I told you about Serge? – was right against it: "You're on the cusp of a major exhibition of your artworks. The *cuthp*! All the critics who matter or who are going to matter will be there. And you're tripping off on vacation? For a whole summer? Do you want to sell *anything?*"'

'Does he really speak like that,' I asked. 'I mean with a lisp?'

'Oh yes. I'm pretty good at impersonating. Especially on the phone, sweetie! "You can't live on fresh air and sea views, hon. We need another dozen maybe. Fourteen pieces – okay – to achieve completion. Time is not on our side." Serge just wouldn't let go. Even though I told him I'd be working down here. "And how will you get the pieces to us? And will they be able to ship it in time?" You should have heard him, Roberto!'

'And this is in Boston?'

'Yeah, the Wilkinson-Mandate Gallery, you won't have heard of it. Oh, sometimes I wish I could just stay here and let them handle everything from their end, but I know I can't trust them. Not even Serge and I've been working with him for ten years now. The little shyster!'

'What does that mean? Shyster?'

She patted my thigh. 'I don't know, Roberto, maybe, charlatan? Anyway, as soon as I said I was going, they all wanted to know when I would be getting back. As if they were going to mark up their diaries and until then I no longer existed. I wasn't even gone and already they wanted me home. Well, I was bored of the studio, the people I saw, bored of the scene, the bitching, backbiting. You've no idea, Roberto... artists are just the worst! I just wanted to get on a plane. Be somewhere uncomplicated. Somewhere by the sea. Then I knew it had to be here. Back to my friend Robert!' She squeezed my thigh and I felt that I was blushing and something else was happening.

'Of course, I'm just so lucky,' she continued. 'That I can do it, just take off. My line of work is seasonal you see and I'm building up to an annual selling show in the autumn. But there's a waiting list for my pieces, especially the bronzes, so I don't know why Serge has got to make such a fuss. All I have to do is create and after a year of that you find you need to clear your head, get some fresh air into it. That doesn't come if you sit inside four walls day on day. Are you falling asleep?' She giggled in my ear.

'Me? No, no, I was...'

She gave me the most gorgeous smile, close up. I longed to kiss her. 'That's okay, Roberto. I go on rather. Me, me, me...'

'And Big J?' my voice had shrunk to a whispery croak. 'What happens when you have to go back?'

'I don't know,' she smiled. 'What should happen?'

'Well... I don't know.'

'Neither do I,' she smiled, putting her arm around me and squeezing. 'That's the beauty of it, I guess.'

* * *

I wasn't getting anywhere with Tara. Maybe this was because I was preoccupied with the greater passion of Xanthe and Big J, or maybe because I knew the end was near and it didn't seem worth the bother. We took little strolls and I was like a tourist guide or an anthropologist. I had barely kissed her and those were little more than empty gestures, perhaps philanthropic on her part, experimental, certainly perfunctory. One day I took her into the Seatown.

'They're all so *tiny*,' she exclaimed as I led her through the tangle of narrow slipways and intersecting tracks, compounded into clay steps. 'About five feet high. And painted such bright colours.'

'But they've all got big-screen TVs inside.'

'Have they?' She looked disappointed. 'Look at these model boats in the window! Do you think they carved these themselves?'

'No. I'm afraid not.'

'These little sort of still life scenes: arrangements of shells and other things. Isn't it dinky?'

'It's dinky,' I agreed. 'And maybe a teensy-weensy bit twee, no?'

'I like them.' There was this I disliked about her; a resistance to ideas, to original thinking. She was obstinate, her thoughts were dull clichés. Maybe this was why I couldn't be full on with her. It wasn't her mind I was interested in of course. I had a headboard without a single notch on it.

'Don't you feel there is an inwardness about the place?' I inquired. 'Few have a sea view, for example. They're all built gable on to the sea. You can understand why. The sea is such an ever-present threat that it needs to be hidden from. Look—' I touched the smoothed bright yellow walls. 'These are thick. Maybe two feet thick in places, and the doorways are like the entrances to rabbit hutches.'

'They're cute. Look at these handrails running along the walls. This one even goes over in front of the windows.'

She was very keen on the big anchor. 'But how did they get it here?' She peered at the people passing by on their way to the sands. I could make out the muttered accents of England and America. They came from far and wide to gawp.

'You see that all the doorways open to the east or west side, none open to the north. It's like they don't want to have a view of the sea.'

Tara discovered a carving I had never seen before. Above a lintel and a blue door, it read: 'Time will be forgot, eternity is all'. 'But what does it mean?' she pleaded.

'I think it belongs to the church maybe. Or one of the old churches that used to be here.' I told her, and then I remembered. 'No, it's from a gravestone. There was a huge flood in the 1950s and there used to be a graveyard here and all the stones were flooded.'

'Cool!'

'Most of the graves were never found.'

I thought I might get a chance for a snog if I took her out of the village so I led her along the shingle. I was praying that Breeks wouldn't appear. I knew what would happen if he saw Tara. We walked along to the gap in the cliffs where the grass slope began beside the solitary red obelisk called the Maiden Stane.

'Why's it called that?' she asked looking up at it. 'Look at all these, like, pebbles stuck in it.'

'Old red sandstone,' I told her. I didn't take my eyes off her tight bottom in the faded jeans. 'When the Vikings came, they loaded their ships with slaves and one woman refused to leave her slaughtered husband's corpse so they killed her on top of it.' She seemed to believe it. I had no idea whether it was true or not. It sounded plausible. Although she kept asking questions, I knew she was only feigning interest and I knew I was forcing myself into the role of know-all, boring her to death with facts, and making our relationship ever more academic, ever more distant from emotion and passion and physicality. A little voice inside my head kept telling me the only way out was just to grab her and kiss her to death. It was the only way. I began to lay out my strategy in my mind; where would be the best place for an ambush?

A track leads to the old limekilns. She couldn't get over the fence. I had to hold down the wires so she could squeeze through.

'Look at my jeans!' she complained. 'I got mud on them.'

I turned away. If there's one thing worse than a whingeing girl I hadn't found it. 'Come on!' I called. Sometimes Tara was a child, other times she was just a mixture of desirable and horrible. I told her the story of the séance and tried to make her laugh about the horned one. She took it seriously.

'But don't you, like, believe in the occult and superstition and such?'

'Not when there's a goat involved.'

I took off my jacket and spread it on a flat piece of grass in front of the ruin and sat down on one side. 'Smoke?'

She stood in front of me and looked dubiously at the ground. 'Is it all right?' she asked. 'No creepies or ants?'

'Not as far as I can see.' I began to roll up a joint. She sat down beside me and watched.

'Xanthe's having a barbecue on Saturday,' she told me. 'You're coming. And that friend of yours... Jay, is it?'

'Big J.'

'Yeah. Xanthe must like him a lot to have him there in the house, with Oliver there too. What does he do?'

'He's a poet.'

I could tell she wasn't interested. 'Very young to be a poet. Don't they have like, beards and such?'

I didn't reply immediately. 'He's had loads published,' I finally told her.

'I mean, he is quite cute. He looks like a New Romantic. Except for the leather jacket of course. But you can't hear what he says, he speaks so soft. The first time I saw him I thought he might be gay.'

'He's not. He's had loads of girlfriends.'

'Has he ever been in prison?'

'That's a funny thing to ask.'

'Xanthe really likes him, right, but there's something... I don't know... maybe dangerous about him. Like he gets in lots of fights.'

'He doesn't do that stuff. I mean, not now.'

'Anyway, it's going to be interesting seeing him and Oliver together.'

'Yeah.'

Apart from the oystercatchers and some vertical drifts of dancing flies by the entrance to the limekiln, nothing was moving. Even the clouds seemed to stand still. I thought about the inwardness of the Seatown, the eyes of the folk averted from the greater danger of the sea, and watched a tiny drop of dew drip from the yellow furze of the ragwort. The silence was absolute, a tiny fragment of perfection, scented with drying seaweed and fresh grass and dandelions, wild garlic.

'Oh God, it's so quiet!' she exclaimed. She handed me back the joint and lay down – bare arms cradling her head – with an imperceptible sound of enjoyment. Her eyes closed. I studied her face; the pert nose, the wet pink gash of her mouth, slack and available. The silky feel of her short platinum blonde hairs. For a long minute I watched my shadow gather across her chest then I moved slowly down to her mouth. When I put my lips on hers there was a little electric buzz, static, that surprised both of us. Gentle at first, then wetter, hotter, we ground our mouths together, tongues wrapping over each other, around and behind the teeth. We searched each other's mouth thoroughly and it soon became boring. After a few minutes of this I began to make my moves. I did everything very slowly. I put my left hand onto her stomach just under the hem of her tee-shirt, on bare warm skin. Eyes closed, we still searched the crevices of each other's mouths. After a while I tried to disengage but every time I moved, Tara's hot mouth found mine again. Meanwhile, my hand inched upwards and found the impenetrable wire of her brassiere. My fingers faltered, our mouths and tongues sought each other; I slipped two fingers under the wire and pushed the cup upwards.

'Ow,' I heard her say faintly.

I slid my palm up over her breast, wobbling the nipple. I opened my left eye and took a quick peek. Her breast flopped whitely upon itself, the sunken nipple wide and pink. I attempted to lift my head over to it but her hand forced my head back. Kissing – that's all she wanted to do. After a few minutes of stroking the jellyfish, I took my hand away and moved to the zip of her jeans. Very quickly and firmly her hand grasped my wrist and moved it back to her breast.

'I like that,' she murmured. 'Ooh.'

And that's all that happened. After a while, she sat upright and pushed down her tee-shirt. I sat up. I was all wet and sticky.

'Nice,' she said softly. 'I like kissing you.'

I put my arm around her and tried to push her back down but she resisted.

'You're too eager!' she said warmly. Then we began kissing again, sitting upright this time. Later, I rolled another joint and she began blabbing about her schoolfriends and what bitches they were and that killed the mood. The snogging was finished. We walked back.

* * *

Saturday started fair and by midday there wasn't a breath of wind and even the old folks down at the Braeheid had discarded several outer layers. Even Shopsoiled Susan was seen to smile but that might have been because she had managed to cheat a customer in change. Sandy Stokes brought his deckchair to the entrance of the Beach Café and sat there grandly in his shirtsleeves, smoking rolly-ups. Flocks of tourists strolled in cardigans on the pier. The tide was so low the few small boats lay keeled over in rapidly paling mud in the harbour and the seaweed-strewn rocks seemed to reach far out into the bay.

'Where are you going mannie, a' dolled-up?' Hecky wanted to know. He sat on his front-step and squinted up at me. 'He's no in.'

'Haven't seen him for ages,' I said.

'Me neither, lad. It's this school play.' He shaded his eyes under his battered hand. 'Hope he's no turning out to be one of they thespians!' He thought this was a good joke and I could hear him still chortling and coughing as I turned the corner.

'Robbie!'

I looked around. It was the old lady from two doors along, Mrs Pettigrew. 'You'll be going to the blackenin the day? Young Swye's getting spliced the morn, ye ken.'

'I can't make it,' I told her. 'Going to a barbecue.'

'You enjoy yersel laddie!'

I started up the Braeheid to the bungalows. In the distance, somewhere in the New Ground, I heard clamour and banging, shouts and jeers and a roaring engine. That would be Swye Ironside's prenuptials. We have this tradition in Dounby. Some of your mates kidnap you and stick you in the back of a bogie and tow you about the place after covering you in oil and feathers and whatnot, shouting and drinking and carrying on. Needless to say the Social Worker is dead against it but there's nothing he can do. It's a tradition of the place. I didn't know Swye that well – he was in his mid-twenties – but that usually didn't matter. It was a good excuse for drinking. Then I thought of Xanthe and hurried up.

I had brought a large bottle of dry cider with me. It was the best I could do, being only seventeen – and known to be – for miles around.

At the top of the brae, the beauty of that summer's day was more obvious. Yachts tilted luxuriously on the stippled water. The grass on the hillside was delicately tinted with broom, dandelions, red poppies, and blue speedwell. You could hear the distant wash of the incoming tide.

I knocked. There was no answer and my heart sank but the door was open so I decided to go in. I called, but there seemed to be no one about. They were outside in the garden. Of course they were! I felt foolish being in the house without permission and slipped back out of the front door then went around the side into the garden.

Tara reclined in one of those aluminium structures that support a sun-bed. She was wearing a gold and silver bikini that seemed too small for her and a large straw hat. She didn't see me until I was up close. I saw that she had her Walkman on.

'Oh, hi!' she chirruped. 'How're you?' Then she plucked my sleeve. 'Oliver's in a foul mood. Something Xanthe said apparently. Something about *him*.'

I kneeled beside her, examining how the upper part of her breast lapped over the tight rim of her bikini top like liquid. She smelled of coconut oil. 'So he's here is he?' I whispered. Somehow I had convinced myself Big J would not come. Nor could I really believe she would invite him. There seemed only one reason why she would. I didn't know how I felt about that. 'And Oliver?'

Tara pointed to the conservatory. Oliver was deep inside the cane chair; his meaty arm overhung it while his other arm manipulated the telephone close to his face. He looked overheated and choleric. I could only catch certain words, abrupt, crude language. I saw Big J and Xanthe on the edge of the lawn under the trees. J was tending the barbecue in a haze of blue smoke. The exquisite aroma of charring meat assailed the air.

'Robbie!' Big J waved. They seemed to be standing unnaturally close together but maybe I was a little oversensitive to that.

'Oliver's deal has fallen through,' Tara said. 'Or at least that's what it sounds like. I hate him when he's like this.'

'Let's go over,' I suggested.

'You go. I'm sort of stuck in this sun-bed. Did you bring any... you know?'

'Maybe. And maybe not.'

I walked across the lawn. There were two other people there; their faces were vaguely familiar to me, sitting on a bench beside the shed gazing out on the view. They both wore white suits and held up tall cocktail glasses.

Xanthe was her casual self in tight khaki shorts which took your breath away and a white tee-shirt that seemed to form around her breasts. She was barelegged and her toenails were painted cerise. She had never looked more gorgeous.

'Robbie – you know Mr and Mrs Rumbold?'

'Oh, Dennis and Anne, please!' protested Mr Rumbold, a weedy looking man with overwashed black hair and a scrawny neck. The wife was plumper with thick spectacles. They were summer visitors, owned a cottage nearby. Incomers. I had no idea why they were in Xanthe's garden.

'I've seen you, I think.'

I was favoured by a cheery smile. 'You're one of our bright chaps who's going off to University soon, I gather. Well done, sir!'

Mrs Rumbold adjusted her spectacles to consider me closely. Her voice was dry and sarcastic. 'And, may I ask, which particular grove of academe you are intending...'

I talked to them politely for a few minutes but out of the corner of my eye I was closely observing Xanthe who was dreamily gazing at nothing on the horizon. I had conceived a desperate plan whereby I would prevent the catastrophe ahead by declaring myself to her. Under some pretext, I would lead her indoors and trap her in the bedroom and ravish her. Then Big J would shrug bravely and say 'the best man won' and I would tell Oliver to leave. I had it all worked out. Not.

Under the pretext of helping with the barbecue I sidled over to Big J. He wore cut-off jeans, whose white threads straggled over his heavy dark-haired thighs and a blue-and-white-hooped tee-shirt. He looked like a pirate. 'Word of advice, Rob,' he said softly. 'Steer clear of the English bull.' He looked at me, smiled and nodded. 'I'm probably going to have to smack him if he speaks to Xanthe like he did earlier.'

'Whee!' I exhaled. 'I need a smoke.'

'Me and all. Got some?'

I nodded.

'Well, but not now. It's just the kind of excuse he needs.'

'The steaks look great!' I said loudly since I could feel Oliver's presence behind me.

'Christ, chummy!' he roared. 'Watch what you're doing!' He made a grab for the tongs but Big J turned and evaded him.

'What is it?' J asked innocently. Oliver had nearly slid into the flowerbed. He got up with the snarl still on his face.

'Laddie, I've being organising barbecues since before you were born.'

'Yeah?' J queried with that sarcastic look. 'So what?'

'Why don't we all sit down?' Xanthe cooed, pointing to the arrangement of white plastic seats grouped loosely around the table at the edge of the lawn overlooking the bay. 'Elspeth will bring the drinks out.'

'Who's Elspeth?' I asked J.

He nodded at the conservatory. 'She's with them – the Rum Coves.'

I laughed. 'They have a daughter called Elspeth?'

'My favourite name,' J said. 'Xanthe and I – we'll call our daughter Elspeth.'

'No, you won't.'

'You're right. We won't.' He poked at the steaks. 'Oliver wants his blood-rare,' he observed. 'Isn't that typical? That man is a boor.'

'As for the Rumbolds – I'm surprised they eat meat at all.'

'They're cannibals, Robbie. Only eat their own kind.'

Our laughter drew Xanthe back over. 'You two! Come over and sit down. Be sociable.' I saw the secret smile she gave him and longed for it to be mine.

'Come on, let's go over.'

Elspeth came out bearing a silver tray of tall drinks. She was tall and emaciated, her skin stretched too tightly across her nose. The full-length floral dress hung on her like a half-drawn curtain.

'Drinky-poos!' she cooed. She saw me and beamed. 'Fresh meat!'

For a fraction of a second, I remembered what J had told me about the Rumbolds. Could it be true? I squirmed in my seat.

'Cocktails, everybody,' Xanthe called. 'These are the alcoholic ones.'

Oliver grunted. 'Some of us aren't old enough to be drinking alcohol anyway.' I glanced at him. Was he meaning me? He couldn't be. He was the one who had taken me to a pub. 'Or barely,' he added grouchily. The laugh of it was that it was the three Rumbolds who were reaching for the non-alcoholic ones.

'Never touch the stuff!' Dennis Rumbold said brightly. 'I'm best friends with my kidneys.'

'I heard a good one the other day,' Oliver boomed. 'Down in the Norseman. Chap there called Sid Fyves, old fishing sort, you know. Says, "If I try to drink whisky with water I boke." That's local dialect for vomit, y'know. Anyway, "I get the two flavours mixed," says old Sid, "whisky's for you, the water's for your kidneys."'

'That's a good one,' said Dennis Rumbold, 'the water's for your kidneys, the whisky's for you.'

Big J and I exchanged a mocking glance.

'Don't go down there often, of course,' Oliver said. 'Sometimes the locals can be hostile to a chap. Eh? What the bloody hell's that racket?' He stood up. 'Bloody hell!' We all got up. On the main road, half a dozen youths in the back of a flatbed truck were beating sticks on the bottom of metal fishboxes and the side of an oil drum. I recognised Rob and Ed among the others and Swye Ironside – face blacked up – and waved.

'Friends of yours?' Dennis Rumbold said. 'Oh dear.'

'It's a blackening,' I explained. 'The chap with the greenish hair, see, he's getting married tomorrow.'

'I see…' he said and plainly he didn't. 'Do they have to make such a noise about it?'

'It's the tradition.'

'The natives are bloody revolting,' Oliver exclaimed in a pompous voice. 'Bloody jungle drums! They want us out. Total Independence!'

'Don't be stupid!' Xanthe said. I looked at her. I could hardly believe the vehemence with which she had said it. Big J was grinning. Oliver barely moved at first. He lolled in the chair and took a deep draught.

'I'll pretend I didn't hear that,' he said finally. The Rumbolds looked acutely embarrassed. 'I mean,' Oliver said reasonably in a silky sort of voice, 'we are incomers, some of us don't pretend otherwise.'

Xanthe looked at him and put down her glass. There was an unbroken moment of silence then Tara burst in on the group.

'Hey, who's watching the steaks?'

J leaped up and sprinted over to the barbecue.

'At least Elvis knows his place,' Oliver grunted. 'Get back in dem kitchens boy, rustle up de grub for dem massas.'

'Do you think he looks like Elvis?' Tara asked innocently.

Oliver snorted. 'Tight arse and grease in his hair…'

'You're just jealous,' Xanthe said with a genial smile.

Oliver exploded. 'Jealous?' he roared. 'Of that young greaseball?' He was on his feet, swinging his red fist in front of his face. 'Do you think I'm blind? Do you think I can't see what's been going on...?'

The Rumbolds stood up as one. 'I think, maybe... we...'

'Sit down!' Xanthe snapped. 'Oliver is going to calm down. Or Oliver is going to leave.' She glared at him. 'Isn't he? Which is it? Oliver?'

'I'm sorry,' Oliver said throatily, his face congested. He sat down, tried to smile. 'Too many of these maybe. Yes.' He tried to make light of it. 'Not good for the kidneys, no.' He smiled with an attempt to put everyone at their ease and then sank straight into a deep sulk. One by one everyone, affected by his mood, slunk away and reassembled over by the barbecue, suddenly absorbed by the intricacies of the coals, the condition of the meat, the need to check the cellophane covers in case flies had got in to the salad or the buttered rolls.

Tara stood close and I felt her arm come around my waist. 'Got any?' she whispered. I nodded.

'When'll it be ready?' she asked.

'Not long,' J told her. 'Five minutes. To be on the safe side.'

Tara led me into the house by the back door and through the corridor into her bedroom. 'Don't get the wrong idea,' she cautioned. 'Just for a smoke, yeah?'

Truth to tell, I felt very tense. I was too preoccupied with what was happening with Xanthe and Big J to be interested in her. Even the dope failed to chill me out. In fact, I was so cool about it that I just watched while she stripped off her bikini bottoms and pulled on a pair of white panties and lycra leggings over the top of them.

'Least I'm not having to fight you off,' she said dully.

'Sorry. It's the tension out there,' I told her. 'Getting to me.'

'Like, do you think they're going to fight?'

'I hope not. J would molocate him.'

'Maybe. My uncle's pretty powerful. He was in the army, you know. In the Falklands. When he gets in a rage...'

'Let's hope it won't happen. Come on, Tara, those steaks will be ready now.'

When we went back out, everyone was sitting down to eat. Elspeth was pouring out fresh drinks. Things seemed to have calmed down a bit. Except when Tara said, 'Why don't we have some music?' And Oliver sneered, 'Maybe something by Elvis, eh?' But that was easily glossed over. Everyone was too preoccupied with their food and keeping a watch out for flies. In the distance, we heard the continuing clamour of Swye Ironside's blackening, but no one remarked it. It had got rather hot, conversation lapsed. Xanthe was sitting next to J and I suspected her hand was straying to his thigh now and then but I couldn't be certain.

'We're supposed to be going into Duncairn this afternoon,' Xanthe told everyone. 'There's an open-air concert in the Summer Park. We're meeting Nicol and June there.'

'Nicol and June,' Oliver groused, rolling his eyes.

'You usually like them,' Xanthe soothed. 'They have a daughter Tara's age,' she informed us. 'Goes to the riding school. That's how we met.' Her eyes met mine. 'Maybe you'd like to come with us?'

J and I exchanged glances. I could see that it had been prearranged somehow. I could also see that Oliver wasn't keen.

'Tara's coming anyway,' she added.

'Too right! Get away from this place,' Tara asserted. She touched my wrist. 'And you'll come too, won't you, Robbie?'

'Yeah, okay.'

'Don't sound too happy about it,' she riposted.

Xanthe laughed lightly. 'The more the merrier. I don't think Oliver wants to come.'

'Oliver can bloody well speak for himself!' he snorted.

'Xanthe's voice was almost plaintive. 'You said you weren't going to. Make up your mind.'

'We won't be going of course,' Dennis Rumbold said. Talk about stating the obvious!

'No, I wondered if you wouldn't,' Xanthe said politely.

'Far too trendy for us,' Anne Rumbold offered. 'We're not gay young things any more.'

Tara sniggered into her napkin.

'Unless you want to go, dear?' Dennis Rumbold asked Elspeth dubiously.

She shook her head, mouth full of ice cream. 'N...uuuhn.'

'Didn't think you would, dear.'

Oliver produced a cigar. I suspected from the distaste on the faces of the Rumbolds that this had been discussed earlier. He disregarded their nervous looks and lit up. I may have imagined it but he seemed to puff a lot of the smoke in their direction. They visibly shrank in on themselves.

'Nothing like a good cigar,' he ventured wilfully. 'Second only to good sex.' He glared at Xanthe. 'Isn't that right, dear?'

'If you say so,' she responded coolly, her eyes coincidentally wandering to the advancing figure of Big J. I saw that glance and so did Oliver. He started. Went red in the face.

'Are you all right?' Tara asked her uncle in alarm.

'Went down... the wrong way...' he spluttered, getting to his feet.

Big J stood there coolly, a slight smile playing on his open features. He was remarkably well tanned, given that sunshine in Dounby had been almost nonexistent until very recently.

'Drink water...' Oliver said, barging into him. It was deliberate of course, and J's food went onto the grass. J stood looking after him.

Xanthe made a space for him at the table. 'Never mind him,' she said. 'His deal fell through.'

'What deal?' J asked blankly, picking his steak up gingerly from the grass.

'God knows,' she said, adding vehemently: 'who cares anyway?'

I looked at her. I was unused to seeing this other side of her, this steely resolve. It looked as if she had made a public declaration there and we all knew it. Even the Rumbolds, preparing to make an agreeable exit, knew it.

I felt exhilarated, I felt miserable, didn't know what I felt.

To break the mood, Xanthe stood up, just as Oliver returned. 'Well, if we're going to that concert, we'd better make tracks. We can clear up later.'

'We are going then?' Oliver demanded. Then he held up his big hand. 'But there's one thing you've overlooked. By inviting all and sundry... you've forgotten... damn it, there's too many for the car!'

'Oh no problem,' said J breezily. 'I've got my bike.' Xanthe and J shot each other a blatant glance that was so obvious its import could not be clearer. Oliver realised the awful truth. She intended to go on the bike... and he... would be left to transport Tara and me!

'I see!' he snapped. 'Well, maybe...' he turned and went back into the house.

We stood uncertainly, shaking hands with the Rumbolds. There was some awkward stooping to kiss cheeks and then Xanthe ushered them out by the side gate, and went inside the house. Tara and I walked round to the front.

Oliver had J's leather jacket on. He stood bent over the motorbike. For a ridiculous instant, I thought he meant to attack it. But he straightened up. 'Beautiful machine anyway,' he said. 'Built for these roads. I'm going to ride this machine till it breaks.'

'Don't be ridiculous, uncle!' Tara's voice shrilly expressed our outrage.

'It's not me who's being ridiculous. I've seen them together, her and motorbike Mike.' He glared at me. 'Tell your friend,' he snarled, 'tell him, I'm taking this bike to town. Fair exchange is no robbery. He can go in my car. Can't say fairer than that!'

I rushed back inside to find J. He wasn't in the kitchen or the conservatory. He was in the back hall. He and Xanthe were pushed up against the wall, frenziedly eating each other.

'Jesus!' They broke apart.

'You startled us,' she said.

'He's taking your bike,' I told J.

'He's what?'

I told him again. 'It's no joke. Says you can go in the car.'

'But he's off his face with drink,' J gasped.

Xanthe threw her arms in the air. 'Ah, let him!' she said. 'He's impossible.'

J looked from me to her. 'No way. My bike?'

'He's a fool!' she said curtly.

Then we heard the powerful roar of the bike. We rushed to the window and saw it squirting gravel as it rolled out of the drive.

'At least he's got the helmet on,' Xanthe said. 'Hell mend him!'

As the bike reached the road, Oliver's leather-jacketed arm came up in a slow gesture of defiance.

'Bastard!' J snapped. 'If he totals my bike, I'll...'

* * *

'You're my man,' she said. 'My summer man, in my summer place, ' I heard her say softly to Big J. Her left hand rested in his as she steered the 4x4 with one hand around the bends. In the back seat, Tara and I sat looking out in different directions, disconsolate for different reasons.

'God, if he's in some ditch somewhere!' she repeated anxiously.

'He'll be all right,' I reassured her. 'He's a big boy now.'

'That's just what he is,' Xanthe agreed from the front seat. 'A great big boy. And J here is a man. My summer man.'

Tara nervously giggled.

J was looking pleased with himself, a shade triumphant perhaps. He was hearing what he wanted to hear, no doubt. But it occurred to me then, for the first time, as a kind of cold revelation, that Xanthe needed more than one man. She required many men to deal with her various needs. She had a man in London who does 'this and that' for her. Another guy, somewhere else, handles 'everything' for her and of course, her agent, the shyster Serge, jumps through hoops to keep her name prominent in useful circles in Boston. Men danced around her like flies on shit – that was a fact – and she kept the whole menagerie moving with a flick of her finger. She was always moving, never still... in some magic way, it all happened successfully in her wake... as if she just spread her invisible wings a little. Now she was discarding one man and acquiring another – for the summer – or what was left of it. She moved freely, unscathed among men, and marked her progress using their names like entries in a diary. But it was all done effortlessly, discreetly, and painlessly. The men were willing volunteers, happy to sun themselves in the light of her personal aura. Big J had no idea of any of this. That simple uncomplicated fool was too close to see what I now saw clearly for the first time. Gone were my own cravings for her, cravings of which she was undoubtedly aware, and had been all along. I could see through the wonderful veneer – and my ego would not permit me to be a slave to her. Her attitude to Oliver had struck me as hard, ruthless, as if for her he was already in the past, whether dead or alive. On balance, of course, I couldn't see Oliver coming to real harm. He wasn't the type and the nearer we got to the city, the more I was convinced he had made it through sheer force of will.

'Take the next bend slowly,' J suggested. 'You never know...'

'You don't think...?'

'Slow down... I'll look.'

'Poor uncle!'

J had the trophy for the summer. Her summer man. For him it was almost worth the sacrifice of his treasured bike. He would be magnanimous about it, would forgive Oliver – assuming he wasn't too badly injured. I had often wondered what Xanthe saw in him. I think he *represented* this part of the world for her. She conquered territory by means of the men who belonged to it, or to whom it belonged. Big J was her stand-in for the landscape. By making love to him, she was being accepted; she was becoming Dounby, inhaling its mores, its values. As an artist, she was, by definition, a good thief, had learned the value of novelty and how to extract it purely in its clearest essence. She could see exactly in what way each thing wanted to be a more perfect ideal of itself, could see its ambition, its true form. Everywhere she went she derived new ways of seeing and after she had seen, the places shrivelled back to themselves when she moved on. Hers was exploitation, a temporary agitation of the senses. Like the bumblebee, she moved on, clammy with pollen. These were some of my thoughts at the time that I kept private. I was hoping I was wrong but things were working out like the final act of that tragedy by Bill Shakespeare. There was the smell of something doomed in the air.

By this time, we had reached the outskirts of Duncairn, the neat and nasty terraces, the grey hard stone, the parked cars, double yellow lines, church spires, single teenage mothers with pushchairs.

'Perhaps we should go to the police?' Tara said, her eyes patrolling the side streets, the pavements and parking spaces.

'And say what, dear?' Xanthe purred. 'That your uncle has borrowed a bike and is drunk as a skunk? He wouldn't thank us for it.'

'Where are you meeting these friends of yours?' I asked. 'And does he know where?'

'Oh yes, Oliver knows where,' Xanthe said. 'But he won't be there. He'll make us sweat.'

'The police could look for the bike though,' J suggested. 'In case he dumps it somewhere. You know,' he added, 'if he's got this far, which I doubt. I mean, has he ever ridden a motorbike before?'

'He must have,' I said. 'He didn't have any difficulty taking it away.'

'In the army, he had a motorbike, I think,' Tara said quietly. 'He sometimes talked about it.'

Big J exhaled noisily. 'Oh well! That's good. Maybe get the bike back in one piece then.'

Xanthe gave him a sudden look and although I was unable to see her face, it seemed to startle Big J. 'I think you're more bothered about that darned bike than anything,' she accused. 'I could easily buy you another.'

The roads around the city centre were busy with Saturday crowds and traffic was almost at a standstill. There were several motorbikes but none with the identifiable shape of Oliver on it. At the fourth set of lights, Xanthe turned off down a wide tree-lined boulevard towards the reservoir. The gates to the Summer Parks, a collection of playing fields and nature trails and boating ponds, was at the other end of the road, bounded by a high hedge and fence. We could hear the amplified music as soon as we dismounted.

The public concert was being held in the interior of the park, a large grass area in front of the Pavilion Restaurant and the Botanical Gardens. Someone was shouting enthusiastically through a microphone when we turned around the public toilets at the gate and saw the vast crowd.

'How are we going to know if he's here?' Tara said. 'Did you, like, arrange to meet somewhere specific?'

Xanthe linked her arm in Big J's and half-turned to us. 'By the Pavilion,' she said. 'Nicol and June will be there. We're late.'

'Come on, Tara,' I said. 'Let's get on ahead.'

'Yeah, it's dead embarrassing, isn't it?' she said once we were out of earshot. 'Look at all these people. For Buck's Fizz! I think their music sucks!'

'Will you know Nicol and June by sight.'

'Yeah, if they've got Adele with them,' she said. She clicked her teeth in annoyance. 'Look at them! Love's young dream. If Oliver sees her like that!'

'I thought you told me Xanthe and Oliver were just friends?'

'Did I tell you that? Well… they weren't like, having sex a lot. Hey! Where are they going? Look – they're turning back.'

'Should we follow them?'

'No! Of course not. They want to be alone,' she said sarcastically. 'You can buy me an ice cream. I can't see Adele anywhere.'

8

The strong sunshine, the booming music and the sheer presence of so many people combined to give me a bad headache that made me wish I was back in Dounby by the gentle sea breeze in the shade of the cliffs. Oliver had failed to turn up at the rendezvous and we had waited until the bitter end. We stood miserably at the imposing granite arched gates outside the parks, within view of the car, debating what to do.

Nicol, a prosperous-looking farmer in corduroys and sports jacket, whose face betrayed the effect of too much sunshine and alcohol combined, was trying to calm the situation but every word he uttered seemed to provoke his wife, June, a slim and rather svelte woman with a trim figure which suited her jodhpurs, riding boots and hacking jacket.

'No, no, what I'm saying...' Nicol protested, 'is that we should ring Debbie and Ted... see if he's turned up there.'

'We can't be bothering everyone,' June said firmly. 'Oliver's not a child. We mustn't overreact.'

Xanthe smiled wanly and took little part in the debate. Big J was standing apart from her, leaning against the warm stone, and smoking a cigarette. I wondered if they'd had a row.

Tara was impatient to get home. 'I'm sure that's where he will be!'

'Quite right, Tara. At least someone here has some sense!' June asserted. 'Best thing, beetle off back home.'

'I suppose you're right,' Xanthe said. 'Come on then. There's nothing more we can do here.'

'We could watch for parked motorbikes in the area,' Nicol said, smiling hotly. 'Can't take the buggers into the park.'

'Nicol!' June warned. 'Ladies present.'

'Sorry. Shouldn't have said buggers,' Nicol slurred.

Big J laughed. Xanthe turned to look at him.

'Come on, back to the car.'

There was a definite cooling between them. They had been off by themselves for two hours. When they had come back to the Pavilion, they weren't holding hands any longer. The drive back to Dounby was marked by resentful silences separated by occasional irrelevant remarks by Tara and me. There was no hand-holding in the front this time.

The first thing we saw when Xanthe turned in at the drive was Big J's motorbike, propped up at the front door.

'That's a relief!' Xanthe said.

'I told you this is where he'd be,' Tara exulted.

Xanthe rolled the jeep onto the gravel. There was no sign of Oliver.

'Probably sulking inside,' J said. 'I'd better check the bike's okay.'

'You and that bike!' Xanthe snorted. 'Come on, let's have this out.'

'Perhaps I should be getting home?' I suggested.

She looked at me blankly. 'Maybe better if you stick around for now.' I was glad she'd said that. It made me feel better as if somehow I was her protector, not Oliver, not Big J.

Oliver was in the lounge, reclining in a lordly manner on the sofa, feet up on the pouffe, glass of whisky in his hand. He grinned sheepishly as we entered.

'Well!' Xanthe exclaimed. 'You had us all worried. We were looking everywhere.'

Oliver's head swivelled to take us in. He coughed. 'That's an overstatement,' he said flatly. 'I don't think all of you were worried.' He looked meaningfully at Big J who had entered behind us.

'Bike's all right,' J stated.

'Nice bike,' Oliver said. 'Secondhand I presume, much it cost you, chummy?'

J opened his mouth to speak then thought better of it.

'Never mind the bike, Oliver,' Xanthe said, walking round in front of him and switching off the TV. 'What I want is an explanation. Or even an apology.'

Oliver snorted and quaffed whisky. 'Mud in your eye,' he said unconcernedly. Then to me added, 'Sit down, Bob, there's a good lad.'

'So where have you been?'

'Around.' Oliver's eyes twinkled. 'Went to visit a friend. Bob knows where.'

Xanthe frowned at me. 'Bob – *Robert*... knows?'

It puzzled me too, then, unbidden, Tish's demure face appeared in my mind's eye. Surely, he hadn't...? I froze.

'Yeah,' Oliver drawled, 'friend of mine we met when we were out on the town. That right, Bob?'

I nodded guiltily and my eye drifted to the side to meet Big J's. In front of me, I saw his fists clench. 'You mean you went to see a *prostitute*?' J blurted out. 'While we were at the concert... you visited your hoor?'

There was an absolute silence in which you could hear the clink of the ice in Oliver's tumbler.

'I beg your pardon?' Oliver said, frowning deeply. 'Visited my... *prostitute*? Is this some kind of joke?'

Xanthe sat down on the pouffe. She looked flabbergasted. 'Oliver...?' she began, 'is this...?'

'Of course not!' he rasped. 'Surely you wouldn't believe... good grief! That I could do that...' He turned sharply to Big J. 'Not only are you insulting me by carrying on here... but now this. It's too much. Where did these accusations come from? And why?'

J stepped back, and collided with Tara. 'Sorry!' Then he jerked his thumb in my direction. 'You can't deny it, Olly. A girl called Tish. Robbie showed me where she lives.'

Oliver was very calm. 'Tish? Tish? No, I'm afraid that doesn't ring any bells.'

Xanthe was looking at me. 'Robbie?'

I nodded.

Oliver exploded. 'They stick together. As you might know they would. Preposterous... that I would... and how would he know...?'

'Because you took him there and tried to make him go with her too. That's why!' Big J shouted.

Oliver jumped to his feet and shook his fist. 'This is an outrage! You can see what this is...' he appealed to Xanthe.

Tara was regarding me with a cold, unfriendly stare. 'You went with a prostitute?'

'No, no, I didn't – he did!' I protested.

'This is getting us nowhere,' Xanthe said. 'I want to get to the bottom of this. How do you know where this... Tish... lives?'

'Because he showed me her house,' Big J said, nodding at me.

'And Robbie,' Xanthe was remorseless, 'how did you know the address?'

'Because he... Oliver... took me there on the day we went into Duncairn. I had no idea what was going to happen. He just drove me to the house and she was there.'

'And what happened then?'

'He wanted me to... go with her but I refused.' I felt that I was blushing furiously. The minter of all minters. I looked at my feet. 'He was going to pay. Then he went with her and... later I told him.' I nodded at J who stood hands folded at the door.

'He's a lowlife,' J muttered. 'He beat the girl up too.'

'He what?' Tara shrieked.

'You see?' Oliver said, appealing to Xanthe. 'It gets worse. Such an imagination, these locals. Don't get out much, you see. But this is all balls. There is no one called Tish. Or if there is, I don't know her.'

'Liar!' J snarled. 'Let's all go see shall we? She'll not be able to forget his ugly face.'

It was a stupid suggestion. Having returned from Duncairn no one would want to have to go all the way back again. J was overdoing the outrage. I also noticed that the angrier J got, the calmer Oliver became.

'And these are the friends you've made among the locals,' Oliver jeered at Xanthe. 'Nasty, spiteful youths. I've nothing more to say. I'll be in the pub.' He went out and we heard him close the front door.

Tara was in tears, I noticed. 'The holiday is ruined,' she said. 'I don't want to hear any more.' She hurried out.

'It's true,' J said, walking around the front of the sofa. 'Honest. I could take you to the place.'

Xanthe shot him a withering glance and began to gather up her hair. She was breathing heavily. 'I think you had better leave.'

'What?' J was incredulous. 'You believe that lowlife? That liar? That scumbag who pays women – and beats them up. Instead of me?'

'I've been blind,' said Xanthe coldly. 'Blind to your faults. Now I see things as they really are. Please leave. You too, Robert.'

The tone in her voice left no room for dissembling. At the door, J turned despairingly. 'I'll phone you tomorrow...'

'No!'

'When you've had time to think...'

'Out!'

There is no more miserable sight in the world than a closed door when it separates you from something alive and exciting and worth having. When it no longer offers to open inwards to joy, when it forms an impermeable barrier to your hopes. That was the way Big J and I felt as we stepped down into the gravel facing the short walk to the village. He barely glanced at his bike propped there. It was as if the victor would claim all the spoils or perhaps he felt, because of its recent proximity to Oliver, he no longer wished to claim it.

'I can't understand her, Robbie,' he protested. 'She must know what he's like. I don't think he cares for anything except himself!'

'Maybe she'll realise tomorrow,' I suggested.

'She was leaving him. She was.'

* * *

At about the same time that day, as we were to discover later, an oilworker in a donkey jacket emblazoned with the luminous legend *Xtrol* on the back burst into the smoked glass entrance of the sprawling hospital complex in Duncairn. The look on his face, according to several witnesses at his trial months later, suggested that everyone, even senior doctors in white coats, had better keep out of his way. It always puzzles me how court witnesses are able to remember such details. You have to wonder whether they make it up. There were plenty of witnesses though so they couldn't all have been making it up. Staff in the hospital testified that his orange boiler suit and heavy boots were smeared with fresh oil and grease. They described the man as tall and thickset, whose 'face betrayed great nervous energy clouded with anxiety'. How they knew that I've no idea, although the man they were describing was sitting opposite them in the courtroom. How a face can be energetic I'm not sure, far less how it could be clouded with anxiety. Most court proceedings, it seems to me, are thick with clichés of that sort. There was a statement from his employers to say that he had been helicoptered across seventy miles of sea from the Norwegian sector to Duncairn. His progress through the hospital to the Intensive Care Unit was observed at every turn.

The duty doctor at ICU agreed that the man was agitated. He had barged through the swinging rubber and perspex doors – despite the red-lettered warnings: *No Admittance* – and collided with the doctor, who fell over.

'Don't mind me!' the doctor had shouted, sitting up on his hands. The doctor would easily have remembered that incident and what happened next as well.

The oilman had come to a sudden halt by the Nursing Station and jabbed his finger at the two startled nurses. 'My wife? Where is she?'

They looked up. 'Mister...?' the senior nurse asked.

'Jorgenssen,' the man snarled. His thick accent took the nurse aback. She later suggested that she had thought he might be Polish.

The nursing staff had difficulty understanding him, but when he said his wife's name they led him down the polished gleaming shaded corridor and the sister opened a small room halfway down. Faced with the prospect of seeing his wife, the nursing sister claimed that the change in the oilman's manner was absolute. According to her he had practically cringed at the doorway and meekly followed her inside.

The woman on the raised bed was attached to a drip and he would have seen from the doorway that she had been badly beaten. Large shadows pooled around her eyes and mouth. Her face, scraped of every iota of make-up, looked pale and unhealthy and her hair was pulled severely clear of her face and fastened securely. Photographs were produced at the trial of course to help his defence by claiming mitigating circumstances.

The nursing sister outlined her conversation with Jorgenssen. 'She's been very lucky,' the sister had told him. 'She was found by a neighbour in the street. She was attacked in her home.'

Apparently Jorgenssen seemed to have difficulty in understanding what he was being told. Although his wife was under heavy sedation, he was able to speak briefly to her.

Jorgenssen, it later emerged, was a simple, uncomplicated man. The word motorbike uttered to him by his exhausted wife, together with the idea that his wife had been attacked in their home, set off a chain of thoughts in his mind. His wife had been vague as to the identity of the man and had given him no reason for the frenzied attack. Nor had the police been forthcoming.

'All your lady wife told us,' Detective Inspector Jappy had explained to him, according to his notes, 'is that she opened the door to this madman and that's all she can remember. It seems likely to us that she had been sexually assaulted but she refuses to confirm that.'

Jappy, a ponderous, tired looking man with unhealthily white skin and straggling fair hair was principal Crown witness at the trial. Of course, I didn't attend the trial myself because I was at Glasgow

University by that time but the local newspapers filled many columns with all the details of the case. It lasted four days and my mother kept the papers for me. The police had quickly established that the crime committed at Jorgenssen's house was not a burglary – nothing was missing – and it remained an open case with no suspects.

However, Jorgenssen was a meticulous man, and being already a little suspicious of his wife's behaviour while he was on the rigs, had noted down the number of the motorbike he had seen outside his house door on his last visit home. He had phoned a friend who worked for the police who called him back with the name and address of the licence holder of the motorbike. This friend was never traced and Detective Inspector Jappy strenuously denied that the Police National Computer had been misused. But Jorgenssen had obtained the name and address of the licence holder from somewhere. It had been a long day for him, starting at 5am on the oil rig, changing drill bits during a rainstorm, travelling seventy miles over heavy seas to see his wife in Intensive Care. But now he had the name and address. From what I later learned – or deduced – of his character, I could imagine that having a plan would allow someone like Jorgenssen to sleep well – with sweet dreams of revenge.

* * *

I hadn't slept well and what was worse, my stepfather was going to be at home all day. I was sitting listening to tapes in my room with my earphones on, when my mother appeared in the room. She looked at the usual clutter with distaste.

I took off my earphones. 'What's up?'

'Someone for you,' she said. 'At the door.'

'Who is it?'

She smiled faintly. 'Go and see.'

It was Tara. Looking sweet in a beret and denim jacket with white jeans. She had scarlet lipstick on. Conscious that John was slumped in the armchair in his vest, unshaved, and my mother was baking, I came out onto the step, closing the door behind me.

'You live here?' she said dubiously. 'It's a normal house. I mean, not sort of like the little houses on the hill. I wasn't sure which one it was, but an old lady gave me directions. Is she, like, looking? I can just feel her eyes on me.'

'Don't mind her,' I said, frowning at Mrs Pettigrew. 'The place is a mess or I'd invite you in. Except my stepfather would go berserk if I took a girl into my room.'

Tara giggled nervously. 'Well, I just wanted to speak to you.' She began to play with her hair. 'Not here... can you come for a walk?'

'If you wait a minute I'll get my jacket.' I shot up the stairs and into my room. I found the tinfoil-wrapped eighth of gold Leb. I was wondering whether things might be about to go to red alert. I just had a vague sense of it. So I hunted out the packet of three where I keep them tucked into the mattress. I thundered down the stairs ignoring the grumbles of my stepfather.

'Back later,' I shouted into the kitchen. 'Okay,' I said, swinging my jacket, 'let's go.' I stopped, aware of Mrs Pettigrew watching me steadily through her lace curtains. 'Where?'

'Well, Robbie, would you mind if you came back with me? We can sit in the garden. The atmosphere is terrible. I could do with the break.'

I knew she meant a smoke but didn't want to admit she was only interested in my dope. She was though: I realised then that that was the truth of it. Why I hadn't been able to get close to her, why she seemed to blow hot and cold, act like a kid, then suddenly a mature woman. That thought went right through me. I was fed up of being used. I had no time to ponder it because she began to ask me about Big J. I guessed her questions had come from Xanthe. It seemed to me that they had been having some kind of heart-to-heart.

'I haven't seen him since last night,' I told her. 'He was pretty cut up about it. Why did she do it, turn him away like that?'

'She had no option. She had to. Oliver owns the house.'

'Oliver does? Since when?'

'He always has. It was Oliver she rented it from when she first started to come here.'

'Anyway, even so – what has that to do with Big J?'

'Don't you see...?' Tara started. 'You are a silly...'

But I didn't see. I told her so. She just shrugged and looked sweetly mysterious in that cute beret. The collar of her denim jacket stopped just short of her cheek under the blonde hair which she had spiked up.

'Xanthe never struck me as the type to bother what a landlord said.'

'She doesn't.'

'So, what...? Is she finished with Big J or not?'

'It's very difficult for her.'

I didn't see that. It had been easy enough for her to start the affair and she had seemed to be enjoying it. And with what I knew about Oliver, the surprising thing was that she was staying with him. We had reached the stone dyke at the drive of the bungalow. 'You never asked me anything about Tish?' I said. 'Why not?'

'I don't want to hear about it. It disgusts me. How any woman could sell her body to men...'

'Even to your uncle?'

'He told me all about that,' she said flatly. 'Tish is just somebody he knows through his business. She's not a prostitute. You must have got the wrong idea. He was just taking the mickey out of you.'

'Why would I lie?' I demanded. 'What possible reason?'

'Look, don't start all that again. Let's go into the garden. I'm gasping for a smoke. You have got the stuff with you?'

'Yeah,' I said. 'I suppose.'

'Look, I'd better give you some money. I've been smoking all your dope.'

'Okay. You could buy the next quarter. I'll be seeing Breeks tonight.' The name made her laugh.

'Burr-eeeeeks!'

There was no sign of Xanthe or Oliver about the house so we crossed the lawn to the rough grass behind the line of trees and sat against the rear wall of the old shed, protected from prying eyes by the pile of grass cuttings dried by the sun into orange dust. We had a partial view of the main road and the light reflected off the windscreens of cars and an occasional tractor as they travelled southeast to Duncairn or west to Redstanes.

We didn't talk much and sat apart from each other. I was resolved to make no further pretence of being attracted to her and I was mildly irritated that she seemed happy with that.

'Is this guy Breeks like the main dealer in the area?' she asked once.

'You could call him that.'

'And he can get me a quarter of this?'

'Yup.'

'Cool.' She stood up. 'Back in a minute.'

A few minutes passed. I was relaxed, philosophic. I heard feet mushing the grass. But it was Xanthe.

'Whoops!' I whisked the joint out of sight.

She sat down, smilingly enigmatic beside me, her knees up. Her perfume pervaded me. She put a hand to my cheek. 'Dear Roberto...' she said softly. 'What am I going to do?'

I shrugged. 'I don't know. But I was telling the truth about Oliver and Tish.'

I felt a shudder run through her. 'I don't really want to hear about it,' she said. 'Oliver has told me everything and I've accepted his apology.'

'Oliver admitted it?'

'Oh, yes. Not that I needed him to. He's incapable you know, in that way, you know...? So I knew it wouldn't be sexual, his liaison with...' She frowned. 'There have been a number of previous incidents.' Then she seemed to brighten up. She clasped her knees and smiled. 'Roberto, Roberto, don't look so solemn. It's not the end of the world!'

'And J?'

'Ah!'

'What does "ah!" mean?'

She laughed, and the bright sound seemed to sift through the summer smell of drying grass clippings, pine needles and warmed sea-fresh air. 'You're my special confidante,' she said. I wasn't sure if she was asking or telling.

'I am, Xan— Mrs Pritchard.'

She gave me a teasing look and leaned forward close and suddenly kissed me on the cheek, her hair falling softly into my face. I was astonished and embarrassed all at once. It was what I had dreamed of so often and felt sure she must be aware of. With her I could not be casual and even in such intense moments my gaucheness was a guilty obstacle between us.

'I need to see him,' she whispered. 'I need to explain. Will you tell him? Or better, Robert, can you bring him…?'

'No,' I said flatly. 'I can't.'

She leaned away from me. I was deeply resentful at that moment. Imagining that all her closeness was a ruse to employ me as a go-between.

'Sorry, but I won't.'

'Hmn, Robert, this is not what I expected.' She twined her hair behind her head and shook it down behind her shoulders. 'But you would at least give him a message?'

'Okay.'

'Oh, thank you. You don't know what this means to me.' She kissed me and again I breathed her warm breath. Tara did not reappear which was odd and proved, I suppose, that they were working together. It was Xanthe who walked me to the gate.

'This wonderful weather is giving me a huge desire to work on my art,' she declared. 'You know, I've started two new figures. I intend to work round the clock to get them finished. I'm feeling so creative just now. It's wonderful. And,' she added, 'old Serge will be pleased. He'll be on the *cuthp* of joy.'

Oliver came out of the back door, in shirtsleeves, hands in pockets, puffing a cigar. He seemed embarrassed to see me. 'Bob, old chap,' he muttered, and then he insisted on shaking hands, which I thought very odd. 'No hard feelings, chummy?'

So I had to shake hands with him. Gross! As I closed the gate, I asked Xanthe: 'Is he going away, or something?'

She licked her lip in that irresistible way and looked mysterious. 'Hmn, maybe…'

I started down the gravel path and had just reached the road when I saw movement beyond the gorse bushes on the other side of the road. I had taken a few paces down the hill when Big J suddenly emerged from behind the wall and jumped down to me. He looked pale and sleepless, his hair was uncombed.

'You all right?' I demanded.

'Never mind that,' he said. 'What did she say?'

'She gave me a message.'

'Well, come on!'

'Patience!'

He grabbed my arm. 'Come on Robbie! Out with it!'

'She wants to meet you. On the beach, at 2pm.'

Suddenly his mood changed. He capered down the road, punching the air. 'I knew she wouldn't... I knew it!' Then he was back in my face. 'How'd she seem? Is *he* there?' He seemed to be full of demonic energy, practically crackling with it, restless, hyperactive.

'He is there. But I think he might be going away.'

'Ya beaut!' he exulted. Then he suddenly came to. 'Jesus, the beach at two? It's gone one now. I'd better scoot to get ready. I'll have to get my bike. Is it still there? I hope it'll start. I'll have to have a shower. I haven't any condoms. What time do you make it?'

I had never seen him in such a state. He was practically electric. 'Here, borrow these,' I said, offering him the packet of three.

He barely glanced at them. 'What? Look, I have to scoot. Catch you later, man!'

* * *

With Big J otherwise occupied, I headed over to Alan's place. It had been weeks since I'd spoken more than a few words in passing to my former best mate. I rapped on his door.

'S'me! Robbie!'

'Come in, man!' I heard from the interior. 'I'm in the bog, make yersel a coffee.'

A couple of minutes later, he emerged, shaking his wet hands. 'That was a right minger.' He wafted the air with a newspaper, holding his nostrils with the other hand. Threw the torn newspaper onto the floor by the sideboard.

'Why not buy bogroll, man?' I asked. 'This is the twentieth century after all. Where's Hecky?'

'Out on a trip. No due back till Monday.' He grinned. Why, do you miss him?'

'How's the school play?'

Alan looked mystified. 'What? Don't ask me. I gave that load of bollocks up weeks ago. It was just a skive. Fancy a coffee?'

I stared at him incredulously. 'Skive? After term's ended? That's a new one, Alan. Are you planning to skive off your holidays? Bunk off to school every day like, instead of staying in bed and having a good time?'

'I had reasons. Tell you later.'

'Oh, when? My twenty-first birthday or something? What's the big mystery, man?'

He refused to answer and in the scullery, quizzed me about Big J. 'Saw Ed the other day,' he began. 'He was telling me J's having an affair with some married bint up the bungalows.'

'Yeah, but don't ask me about it.' My turn to be mysterious.

He slooshed milk into the mugs. 'This the same woman whose grass you cut? American lady? Saw her in the Shoprite the other day. Posh or what? Anyway, forget all that – the results are due out tomorrow or Tuesday at the latest.'

'Yeah, so it said on the news.'

'What's wrong with you? Thought you said you'd stormed them? We'll need to be planning a celebration. With Hecky away, I thought I'd have a little party. Just our crowd right, no one from Gardyne – none of the older blokes – just a dozen of us. Keep out the riff-raff. D'you think we should invite Big J?'

'He wouldn't be interested.'

'Everyone could bring their own booze. Breeks'd get us some smoke. I've got loads of tapes. We could clear oot the sofa and put everything in the bedroom. Don't sound so enthusiastic, man!'

I looked around at the dingy clutter of two untidy males. I could see socks overhanging an open drawer that was full of tins of beans. There were squeezed tins of superlager in every corner of the room. Hairs of the wary cat that occupied most of the sofa formed a silkworm trail over the rug and the chairs. 'Let's get the results first. Some of them might have failed. Then – we'll bring in the sanitation department.'

'Look on the bright side then! Me, I'm certain I've passed them all. Hey – wouldn't it be brill if the only one who'd failed was Catto! Wouldn't that be brill? Failed em all. Every single one. Man, I'd piss myself!' We went down the road.

The Beach Café was closed up. A note on the door read: 'Due to a happy event, we're closed until Monday'.

'Happy event?' Alan snorted. 'What? Is Sandy having a baby now or something?'

'Maybe he finally got his car sorted and has went for a drive?' Ed said, appearing round the corner. 'Hi, guys. Thought you'd emigrated.' Following him was Rachel Fyves. We all made with the big surprise, nudge-nudge.

'Aw eh? Something to tell us?'

'Look at their faces! They've been at it like rabbits!'

Then Heather Lowdy appeared too and sanity returned.

'Hullo, Robbie,' she greeted. 'We've just been chatting to the lads off the *Silver Darling*. Alan – your dad'll no be home till the middle of next week. There's a man ill from the other Petrie boat out from Duncairn and Hecky's been asked to fill in when he gets back with the *Iolaire*.'

Alan grinned. 'Brilliant! That settles it – party time. Saturday. My place.'

'Great! Why wait till then,' Ed said. 'The gang's all here!'

'Who're you comin as?' I asked sarcastically. 'The Hardy Boy?'

'Is it fancy dress?' Heather asked.

'Is it buggery!'

When we were out of earshot of the others, Alan said: 'Robbie, next week I've to go into town to do something. Fancy coming with us, make a day of it. Get the early bus in, yeah?'

'Could do. What is it you have to do?' But he turned away smiling. More secrets. Everybody had secrets now. That night, I stood at the back door for a few moments looking at the night sky. It was one of those perfect clear summer nights and the stars were brilliant. It was mild too. I stepped off onto the small square of back green and walked to the wooden table and bench by the concrete wall. I sat there, puffing quietly on the small joint I had rolled out of a single Rizla. There was a faint blue light up on top of the hill where Xanthe's bungalow was, like a star lying in the tufts of grass. I realised it was the arc light from her oxy-acetylene torch. As I watched it, it glowed brighter, then faded, then flashed brighter again. There was no sound, but I knew that she was up there, working at her furnace, creating artworks for her exhibition, manufacturing those bronze men from dull scraps, welding recycled cans and bits of oil drum and rails and old bicycle frames and radiators. I wondered whether fishing boats out in the bay returning from the fishing grounds would be able to see the torch, like a new star above the cliff.

9

There was something about that summer too, some restlessness in the air. Things that had given me ironic satisfaction, things that I could criticise and satirise and jeer and mock, had got beyond even that possibility. Now there was just endless waiting and boredom and anticipation. Even my thoughts of Xanthe and Tara were not sufficient to quell this yearning I had that was the desire for life, the desire to see what lay beyond the next hill. In only a few months I would be away, but the time was going unbelievably slow, it was unbearable, unjust. Whether we all felt like that, or whether it was just my neurosis, I don't recall but certainly there was a new tension in the group. The laughter and mockery on the Braeheid outside the Shoprite was brittle, at times cruel. Those who were to leave were less willing to engage in idle chatter, those who were to stay were keenest to mock to hide their own disappointment. The presence of the sunshine seemed to remind me that for most of the year it was absent. The warmth of the air reminded me how cold it was for most of the year, the familiar chat seemed ever more inanely stultifying. The landmarks were devices to limit my future, the landscape was my prison.

All of my hopes were printed between the lines of a letter from Glasgow University that offered me conditional acceptance to a Chemistry degree course. I had to have at least three Bs, including Maths. The letter, which had passed between my mother, stepfather and various neighbours, was already grey with folding and reading and folding and I kept it with me, in my pocket and every now and then I took it out to re-read. 'Dear Robert Strachan... Yours sincerely, Edward Prestonville, Bursar.' Sincerely. They were sincere. I sincerely believed it. It was a passport to the rest of my life, a one-way ticket out, it afforded me entry to the human race as an adult competitor. The conditions were printed on a separate line: 'require a minimum of three passes at B or above.'

'It's in the bag, no?' Alan said, as we sat on his front step with cans of beer. 'Only three Bs? You did better than that in the mocks.'

'I can't remember any of the exams,' I said. 'Can't even remember being there. For all I know, I could have forgotten to hand in my papers.'

'Come on, man! That's not likely. Anyway, it's party time. Why not go down to Yvie and Lila and get them to come over now.'

I glanced at him. 'You bugger. What you mean is, find out if Lila's had any news of her college place.'

He took a gulp of beer. 'Ach, Robbie, who cares anyway! I've had it with her. I finally realised that she's gone off me. You lot all knew that for ages, I bet.'

'I didn't! Anyway, it's none of my business.'

'We went around for ages, near two years. I told her all that I was going to do and then she started not telling me things. Having little secrets of her own. So tonight, Robbie, I'm going to show her how much I don't care. I'm going to be just normal; I'm not giving her the cold shoulder, no. I'm not going into a huff. Anyway, there's one thing she doesn't know about. And it'll blow her away!'

'You can tell me.' I grinned. 'You've got VD?'

He clicked his tongue. 'Don't joke about that! But this is not a big secret anyway. Remember when I said I was going to help with the school play?'

'Course. You were really after Linda Morrison?'

He made a face. 'Her? Lady Ophelia? No way. Well, what I was actually doing was extra swotting for a bursary comp.'

'What?'

'Aye. Von Blofeld fixed it for me.'

'A bursary? To University you mean?'

'Ho ho. At *Oxford* University, could you imagine, man! Keble College. And I've bloody got it! Two thousand a year and all fees.'

My jaw must have clanged off the pavement. 'But... you never did any work? You never did any work at all! How the hell did you manage it? And why did you no tell me?'

'Wee bit jealousy there?' he queried. He raised his beer can. 'Yup. I'm going to be an Oxford man. Old chep.'

'Bloody hell! *Oxford*? Blofeld must be ecstatic.'

'Well, he doesn't know yet actually. The letter only come this morning. Want to see it?'

'Bloody right! This morning? Jeez, you're calm. Me, I'd be on the bog crapping myself.'

'Hang on, I'll bring it out.' He went inside and I tried to get my head around it. I had hoped we might be going together to Glasgow. I was pissed off. He came back with the letter. 'What's more,' he grinned, 'Hecky doesn't ken anything about it at all. Even that I was putting in for it.'

'You serious, man?' I studied the letter with its imposing crest and list of mega-famous patrons.

'Different worlds, see. I mean Hecky is barely human.' A sudden thought struck him. 'Oh, my God, what happens if there's a parents' day? Shite – can you imagine?'

We had a good laugh. Hecky ponging up the cricket pavilion with fishy wellies. 'I say you cheps, what's thet frightful smell?' Hecky chatting to the Bursar: 'Aye, min, there's a recht swell on the day, a' these toffs gadding aboot.' If somebody tried to shake his hand, he'd probably land one on the guy.

'Aye, because he thinks they're taking the piss out of him and being sarcastic,' Alan said.

'I can imagine that,' I said. 'They'd probably have to get security to throw him out. "Who is this trespasser in the wellingtons?" – "I think he requires the tradesmen's entrance, your lordship?" – "Ah yes, Dean, have him threw out on his erse!" And just imagine if there was champagne? Jeroboams and magnums and flutes of it, on silver trays? He'd waste no time. End up pishing in the silverware.'

'You know, maybe I won't even tell him.'

'You can't keep this secret! Not in Dounby.'

'You're mebbe right.'

'You ken I am. Anyway. Well, congratulations!' I offered him my hand. We shook hands and it was awkward, like we didn't know each other at all. We weren't aware of it but the scale of the opportunities we had each seized already divided us. The enormity of it astonished me. 'A bursary, though! Oxford! God, that's one up for Duncairn Academy!'

'I say, never heard of the place, old chep!' Alan exclaimed in the Lord Snooty accent. 'Somewhere in B... B... Berkshire, what, what?'

'You don't have to speak like that. They must take in ordinary folk too. Anyway, it doesn't sound right when you do it.'

'Give me a week at the place, Robbie boy and I'll sound just like them. Actually no, I won't. I'll still be me.'

'And that's bad enough.'

'Fun-nee!'

* * *

Alan's incredible achievement shocked us but the party was a flop. More like a wake than a celebration. Hardly anybody came, just us. And if the point was to unite us before we all went off, it revealed just how fragmented we already were. To an outsider, it would have looked like a real riot, lots of booze was drunk, everybody got stoned, the sofa got busted, the toilet cistern overflowed, but we knew the group had disintegrated. Nobody wanted to be caught out showing more affection than the others, each of us wanted to be more casual than everyone else. Everyone was desperate to hide his or her real feelings, like you are at that age. So we shouted and jeered and fought and picked on each other. Alan and Lila niggled at each other for hours then their years of going out together exploded in a couple of casual words in the kitchen and she stormed off. Yvie turned up with a stupid guy called Todd, from Redstanes, who didn't fit in. They sat glumly all night, talking to nobody, rolling joints and muttering. Ed and Stuart were bickering about the band. Stuart wanted to go to FE College in Dundee to study music and he wanted to take the name. Ed wanted to keep the band going and replace Stuart. Stuart insisted the band would have to find another name. You'd think they were rock-gods and corporate lawyers! The nub of the argument related to a discussion long ago at the Coble Landing when Stuart claimed – denied by Ed – that he had come up with the name.

'It was me. I'd just been after watching that dumb movie – what was it – ken, the ane wi a' the undead invading a seaside town in America – and that's how I came up wi it.'

Ed swigged his Carlie. 'Na, your memory's well buggered, man. It was me who said the name first. And you weren't even there. Rob... tell him... Rob was with me when it just popped into ma heid.'

'I was just speakin to Josh on the phone the night,' Rob said. 'He says he has a mate who can sort of play the guitar. Can't mind the boy's name the now, but Josh says he might be willin to learn the bass.'

'That right?' Stuart jeered. '*Sort of play?* That settles it. You're no keepin the name. The band is goin right down the tubes. Hey – there's another name for you – The Tubes!'

'Piss off!'

'We'll be able to keep goin. Never you fear, man. We've got two gigs lined up. Mind, you've to play those gigs – if we can't get someone else. You wouldn't want to leave us in the shit?'

'How no? It's where you feel most comfortable.'

'I'm going to smack you in a minute!'

'Dream on, McGugan!'

Rob was applying for jobs in Duncairn and hoping to find a flat there. Rob wasn't nearly as good as Ed on guitar; he was mainly in the band because of his looks. Maybe that was why he kept out of the row. He point-blank refused to replace Stuart.

'Can you no learn a few bass chords, Robbie?' he asked. 'If we get you a lend o a bass.'

'You must be joking?'

'Naw, just really hard up!' Stuart jeered.

'I'll be off to Uni in September.'

'Don't be daft man,' Breeks chipped in, 'you could easy get Lila's job at the Shoprite. Get close to Mrs Small – old Shopsoileds! Then you could be a rock star like Ed. Serious.'

'Breeks? Is this you being sarcastic?'

'It's the dope talkin.'

'You said it!'

'Oxford, for f***sake! *Ox-ford?*'

'Ken. It's a real stonker, eh?'

'Maybe that's how Lila's so pissed off? Al goin to Oxford. And her no.'

'Lila's gone all arty anyways, man. Full o hersel. Just cause she's doing English. She was layin off the other day about *the* Byronic Male. Says Big J is *a* Byronic Male figure.'

'Mo-ronic male figure more like.'

'Why's Big J no here anyway? He should be here.'

'Did nobody tell him?'

'Have you no heard? What happened, I mean?'

'The American woman?'

'Dumped him!'

* * *

I knew where I would find Big J. Everyone had heard by that time what had happened. There were mixed feelings. Some felt he had had it coming, other were more blasé but there was something awe-inspiring about the way he was taking it. He had moved out of his council flat to get more privacy. Disappeared.

I set off after lunch the next day. I had taken a rucksack with a large plastic bottle of dry cider and two packets of tobacco and papers and a small lump of Breeks' finest.

I hit the track that leads around the cliffs and inhaled the fresh warm air. I was swinging my arms and looking all around me, taking huge breaths. It felt good to be out alone. A slight wind scattered the glimmering brine and darkened its patterns under a few incoming clouds. I passed the old seadyke built at some remote time to hold back the descent of soil and grass from the crumbling jumble of rocks above a narrow chasm. I looked down on the Maiden Stane where a few shags waited for the tide to run, tails up, quarrelling like ancient mariners. I reached the open moorland studded with embedded rock and skirted outcrops of gorse from which drifted the faint scent of coconut. I stepped over the old slack wire fence and onto the road. There was no fence on the other side just short windswept grass and then the cliff edge. I stood there, shading my eyes against the glare. I could only see the far part of the beach.

I started to descend. A few pebbles started from their niches and preceded me down the track. Halfway down, I leaned on a fin of rock and saw Big J's shelter, a rough shack at the top of the beach about halfway along. There was no sign of him.

I jumped lightly onto the sand and took off my trainers and socks and rolled up my jeans. The luxury of bare feet on warm sand. I began to trudge my way along to the shelter. There was no movement. But he was here all right.

'Hullo!' I shouted. 'You in there? Big J?' No answer. I had a look inside. It was a rough wooden frame covered with a heavy green tarpaulin. Inside there was a mattress on two wooden pallets. An oil lantern hung from a stake made into a cross frame. I wondered how long it had taken him to get it all down here. Part of me was envious. It was a den, a place where he could be by himself. I pulled up a polythene sack and sat outside the entrance. There was a battery radio. I switched it on. The music was okay so I began to roll a joint. Half an hour went by. I decided to give him another ten minutes before starting back. Then I saw him in the hazy distance, looking very slim, very brown. He had a fishing rod over his shoulder. He had been fishing off the shelf of Auld Darkney.

'Hi!' he called a way off. 'Robbie.'

'How you doing J? Hey, you've got fish?

'Just a couple wee podlies, man. I'll have them for my tea.'

'I've brought you some dope.'

He looked down, grinned. 'Man with dope always welcome in my home. And what's that? Cider!'

After putting the fish into a tupperware box, he sat beside me after a while and we talked, or he talked, in his soft-voiced manner, those far-seeing eyes sometimes regarding me, more often the distant sea.

'So you becoming a beach-bum or something?' I asked gently.

He shrugged and handed me back the joint. 'Aw, man,' he said wistfully. 'That Xanthe. Got me all confused.'

'She makes stick-men,' I told him. 'You should see them; they've got, like, penises too. They're great. She gets two grand for each one.'

'Yeah. I knew that. She's well respected in the art world.'

I just couldn't leave the subject alone. I blathered and babbled like a star-struck groupie. 'She has her shed all done up like a forge. You should see her in there, in her tee-shirt and dungarees. She wears a leather apron. It's amazing, like a scene from hell, all the flames and the heat and the blue flashing light of the torch. She opens the door of the furnace thing and stands there with these huge mitts on then pours out this molten metal into the cast. You should see her figures, they're brilliant. She showed me two. I didn't know where to look because... guess what? They've got genitalia, yes, huge bongs.'

He was more silent that usual. I began to feel his pain by some process of intuition.

'She's wonderful,' he murmured. He thought for a moment. 'Powerful,' he added. 'A sort of post-modern mermaid.'

'A *what?*'

He laughed lightly. 'I wish...' he said. I didn't understand him. But he said no more. And I kept blabbing.

'Heard about Alan? Got into Oxford.'

'Good for Alan,' he said blankly. Then after a moment, added, 'No, I mean that. Good for him. The boy done good.'

'Good dope, isn't it?'

'Hmn.'

'So, what happened... I mean, what did Xanthe...?'

'No, Robbie, if you don't mind... I don't want to talk about it. Not just yet. You understand? Let's just sit and enjoy the karma of this place. Kind of puts everything into perspective.'

After a couple of minutes of silence I grew uncomfortable. 'Your bike,' I said. 'Is it all right up there?'

He turned his melancholy eyes to me. 'Sell it, could you? Keep the money.'

'I can't do that!' I protested. 'It's yours... the papers and stuff...'

'I'll give you the keys to my flat. Get the papers, keep it, sell it, whatever.'

'Man? Your bike...?' I lapsed into silence. We sat there like ghosts in a graveyard. The tide was a distant murmur; even the seagulls left us alone. I wanted desperately for him to jump to his feet and shout: 'Let's play some footie!' or 'Race you into the water, man!' or something... anything. I wanted him to break free of whatever sadness was sapping his spirit. I decided to leave. I couldn't sit with him like this. I didn't want to leave him like this. His life seemed to be ebbing away into apathy.

'Are you going to sleep here tonight?'

He appeared not to have heard me. I repeated the question. It seemed to temporarily rouse him from his lethargy.

'Ah yeah, man. I'll say. It's fabulous. Should have done it long ago. You can sleep like a...' He paused, thinking... 'Like a...'

We both heard the tiny sounds of stone clacking on stone and looked round. There was Xanthe in the distance slowly descending the cliff path. Big J leaped to his feet. 'Oh God, man! I can't face her. You'll have to talk to her. I can't see her.' I couldn't believe it. His hands were shaking. He was a bag of nerves. Standing up, sitting down again. He went into his shelter and when he came out he was wearing a different tee-shirt. 'God, I should have had a shave!' he wailed. I had never seen him like this.

'You look all right,' I said to reassure him.

'Only all right? I need a wash. Do my hands smell of fish?' He thrust them under my nose.

'No, they don't. Calm down.'

'You're right. You're right!' Then he was up again, on his feet. 'I'd better go to meet her. Should I go over? Or wait here?' He sat down and looked at me. 'What do you think?' Then he began to play with his hair, twisting that strand that hung over his left ear round and round in his agitation.

'Hi, boys!' Xanthe called.

We waited for her to come up. She was wearing tight khaki shorts and a cropped white top of the type pre-teen girls wore and her hair was loose, a dark glossy mass hanging down her back.

'I'll better go,' I suggested. 'Leave you to talk.'

'No!' he hissed. 'Stay just for a moment or two.'

'Robbie!' she gushed, 'fancy seeing you here!' But her eyes never even saw me. I stood up to offer her my seat. 'Oh thank you,' she smiled. 'So this is it?' she said, admiring the shelter. 'You've done so well!'

'Look, I'd better be getting back,' I said. 'I only came to visit.'

'No need,' Big J said smiling. 'You might as well stay.' He seemed changed out of all recognition. He glowed, exuded sheer confidence. 'You don't mind, do you?' he asked her.

'No, please stay Robbie,' she said. 'What a fabulous day. And you've been fishing?'

I knew I had to go. The intensity of what they weren't saying to each other was so obvious that I couldn't be near them. But it would have been nice if they'd made more effort to ask me to stay. They barely noticed me as I gathered up my rucksack and turned away.

'See you later, old chap!' J called.

'Bye, Robbie!'

I didn't look back until I got about halfway up. Then I glanced back, saw they weren't watching and I stood there, gazing under my hand at the pair of them, walking away, hand-in-hand at the far end of the beach. I had a huge gulp in my throat and found myself making slower and slower progress up the cliff. At the top, the wind ruffled my hair and I watched to see them reappear almost beyond view, at the water's edge. I felt isolated and depressed and sad and I didn't know exactly why.

* * *

Most of what we know about that day comes not from the trial but from the tabloids. Several printed 'exclusives' giving his side of the story, using the 'jilted lover seeks revenge' angle. So we got a pretty good idea what was going through Jorgenssen's head when he did what he did. Those who knew him said he was a meticulous planner. He would work through the details of his plan like a robot. He would have dressed, washed, shaved, eaten breakfast, locked the front door. That was obvious. That he drove to the big petrol filling station at the roundabout by the Esplanade, glanced briefly at the map in the car before leaving the forecourt, was proved by the CCTV footage. He headed for the ring road and the B8760 to Dounby. Jorgenssen was due back on the oil rig the next day. He had been given four days' compassionate leave. Friends said he was generally not aware of overwhelming emotions. By and large, an unemotional man they said. The practical type. He was used to a wide range of problems in his working life. His supervisor testified that he liked to construct a rigid system for dealing with problems. Even the unexpected could be rationalised. That morning, Jorgenssen had been phoned and told that his wife was going to be okay. She had been moved from Intensive Care to a female medical ward. In a week, she would be discharged. But friends said that he believed that it was not right that the person who had attacked her should escape without punishment. He didn't want to understand what had happened, they said. He didn't want to forgive. He had practically shouted that to a startled courtroom. All he wanted, he said, was to put things right. He was not a religious man but he had felt justified in doing what he did.

Jorgenssen's car was a Volvo estate, a practical reliable car that would pass unnoticed in a car park. He admitted that in the glove compartment as he drove to Dounby was the heavy-duty monkey wrench, wrapped in an oilcloth. It was the tool he used most widely in his trade, the one thing he could rely on in adverse conditions, and no doubt the familiarity of the greased steel in his palm soothed him, made him feel in control.

* * *

Alan and I had got up to the main road for the ten-twenty bus. I still hadn't got over the novelty of making that journey without the thought of school at the end of it but that was the joke because that was where we were going.

'It's a lot of bloody hoo-ha,' he complained. 'And you know what? They wanted Hecky to be there. "Please come with your parents." I told him straight off my dad was at sea. "A most valiant occupation," Blofeld said. Like Hecky was a submarine commander or something. Anyway, Robbie, soon as we get finished we can hit the town.'

'I know some bars,' I told him.

He grinned and we looked at each other and we both said the same thing: 'The Mandrake!'

Except for us and an old lady in the front seat, the bus was empty as it jolted and bounced around tight bends. The driver was pursuing some crazed agenda of his own. Raced up behind cars and went far too fast, bumper-to-bumper, then he slowed to crawling pace and built up a queue behind him. Once, he tooted some farmer in a tractor and pulled out, flashing his lights at oncoming traffic.

'Hecky might feel a wee bit peeved that he's missed out?' I suggested.

'Hecky's got no chance of getting into Keble College.'

'He could read Herring Studies or maybe do Haddockology...'

'Cod Psychology!'

'Or Advanced Blatherskite!'

We got off the bus at the usual stop. 'Seen Big J recently?' Alan asked. 'How's he doing?'

'He's built himself a shelter on the beach. Wants me to sell his motorbike. Or keep it even.'

'Sell it? It'd be worth five hundred easy. He said keep it? Bugger me!'

'I think I'll sell it. I mean I can't ride it. I'll put an ad in the *Journal*.'

As we approached the school gates, we could see a small welcoming party.

'Here we go!' Alan muttered.

Von Blofeld and the String Bean and old Doc Fergus and two people we didn't know stood smiling at each other, as though they had been solely responsible for delivering the Oxford bursary.

'Here he is,' said Von Blofeld cheerily, puffing out his chest. 'Here's Oxford's newest undergraduate.' I may have imagined it but his restless eyes somehow managed to miss me entirely. 'Come into the entrance foyer,' he said benevolently waving us on, as if there was a vast buffet there for us and naked dancing girls with garlands. In the event, there was only the Heedie's wife, a skinny woman in a man's suit, with a bouquet of roses that was handed to Alan, who looked entirely embarrassed. He was almost white. I kept well out of the way and observed the charade. The photographer kept moving everyone around, looking through his camera, and then returning them to their original position. Blofeld kept glancing up anxiously to make sure that the school crest would be in the shot. The woman reporter scribbled down the names and spent a couple of minutes chatting to Alan who stood throughout uneasily fingering his left ear.

'This is Mr Strachan,' Blofeld said afterwards to the reporter. 'He's off to – Edinburgh, was it?'

'Glasgow, Mr Bloomfield,' Doc Fergus put in with a kindly smirk. 'BSc in Chemistry, Robert – assuming everything turns out right.' And he winked at me. I'd always liked old Doc. He never talked down to you. This was his last year. He wouldn't be coming back next term. The place won't be the same without him.

'Happy retirement, sir,' I said. 'You've earned it.'

He beamed. 'Thank you Robert, that's very nice of you to say. One does one's bit.'

'Thank God that's over!' Alan said as we hotfooted it down the street. 'Imagine old Blofeld asking us to his study for tea and biscuits? Thank God you came up with a decent excuse. I couldn't think of anything. That reporter was nice, though, eh? Could have shagged that!'

'Maybe that's what old Blofeld was after? Tea and shagging in the study!'

'His wife was there!'

'She'd be washing the cups.'

'God, look at these!' He glared with loathing at the pink roses cramming the cellophane. 'We're like a pair a poofters!' He glanced left and right. 'These have to go pronto.'

'Can't see any bins.'

'Watch this!' His years in the rugby team had clearly not been wasted. He forward passed the pinks in an arc of rose-tinted blur through the open window of the Watson Crescent Sheltered Housing Lounge.

We didn't stop running and laughing until we were breathless and doubled over. Then we walked out to the main street.

'That'll give them something to talk about!' he grinned.

'Yeah,' I snorted. '"Oxford Student Stuns OAP With Bunch of Hardy Annuals". Done for assault and briary.'

'We'll walk in,' he said. 'Keep an eye out for any dames.'

Although it was only half past eleven, we headed straight for a bar when we hit the city centre. I pulled the collar of my denim jacket up and brushed back my hair. 'How about this one?'

Alan glanced at the sign, which read *The Happy Hen*, peered in the glass sworls of the door. 'Okay, let's give it a shot.'

We pushed open the door and entered the winy, smoky warmth of the adult world. There were a lot of customers in, mainly middle-aged or elderly men, almost no women, except the barmaids. Alan, being over six foot, leaned over the bar while I nonchalantly rolled myself a cigarette. There was a sort of yellow light in the bar and no one was remotely bothered about our ages or us. While the barmaid was pouring our pints, Alan grinned at me and made an appreciative face, with his eyebrows raised in her direction.

We found a space by the painted-over window where we could lean and above us, at shoulder height, place our pints after we'd swigged a great gulp of the strong lager.

'Nice pint,' I said, offering him the rolly-up tobacco and papers.

We had two pints in the Hen and spoke to no one. When we came out on the street, we decided to get something to eat. We found a bakery and bought two sausage rolls. We ate them from the paper bags, walking down the street. Hot and greasy. Alan burnt his mouth on his.

'Bloody microwave! Jeez!'

'More beer?' I suggested.

'Let's try the Students' Union? I went there after with one of the guys doing the bursary comp. Should be some lassies there, even though term's finished.'

'You're on, man!'

But there weren't any girls, at least none we could talk to. Nor any at the Arts Centre round the corner.

'Might as well have a pint, while we're here?'

'Not at these prices!'

We wandered about aimlessly, went into Cairn Park, followed a pair of likely looking students – who promptly got onto a bus.

'I know!' Alan said, plucking my sleeve. 'The Botanic Gardens! That's where all the lassies will be.'

It was a long walk, right through the University campus, and by the Halls of Residence, which looked deserted, down a tree-lined, cobbled lane.

'Sure it's this far out?'

'Not far now.'

'I haven't seen one lassie. It'll probably be closed. And I'm desperate for a slash.'

'Go behind that tree,' Alan pointed. 'See – I'll keep watch.'

You know it's the typical thing. No one for miles until you get your zipper down, then a whole horde of females are right there. Like they can smell it when it's exposed to the fresh air. I heard Alan's loud cough, then a fit of coughing, finally he called: 'Robbie!' There was nothing I could do. It went on and on and when I finally zipped up and stepped out from behind the tree, my urine was a positive river whose tributaries joined the Cairn estuary and flowed into the North Sea. The two girls were having fits of giggles, holding onto each other, just a little further ahead.

Alan was trying to convince them I was a water engineer. 'He's fixing a leak!' When that failed he had resorted to announcing he was an Oxford Man. We began to follow them or rather we discovered that where they were going was the Botanic Gardens.

'We're not following you, honest!' I called. 'I'm a horniculturalist!'

'Rubbish!' shouted Alan, trying to slap my face with an invisible kipper. 'He's doing Chemistry!'

Myta from Kenya and Lorraine from Dublin were a real pair of gigglers. Second year Geography students, faced with resits in September – they were supposed to be studying. They had part-time jobs at the same McDonalds and they giggled practically constantly all the way round and back through the Gardens. Even when we all sat down, they barely stopped. Kissing them was impossible. What they found so funny was a mystery to us. And this of course made them giggle all the more. Lorraine reluctantly let me take her hand and Myta let Alan put his arm around her, but that was it. After an hour when we asked them to go for a pint with us, the giggling intensified. They pulled away after letting us have a brief transitory kiss at the gates.

'We have to go to work,' Lorraine explained. 'But thanks anyway.'

'You're very nice,' Myta said, blowing kisses. 'Mwaah! Mwaah!'

'Sure we can't drop you anywhere?' Alan offered. 'We have the Rolls.'

'No, we ate them earlier,' I reminded him.

'We're due at four o'clock, we have to hurry. Bye-ee!'

'Bye!'

'What a shame!' Alan moaned. 'They were okay!'

'Hey – four o'clock? I've got to phone!'

I found a phone booth outside the Halls of Residence. Alan squeezed in beside me and began to make rude noises while I dialled.

'I was just going,' Tara said. She sounded miffed. 'You just caught me. Oliver is loading my stuff now. Like, why didn't you ring earlier?'

'Oh, I did mean to. We had to come into town. Alan had to get his picture taken at the school.'

'Oh right. Oh, well, I'll write to you, Robbie. Send me your address when you're at College.'

'I will!' I was greatly distracted by Alan capering around. We were practically having a wrestling match. *'Get off!'*

'What's happening? Are you all right?'

'Yes, okay. How are you? I mean, are you glad to be going home?' I had to clamp my hand over the phone because of the rude noises Alan was making.

'Cut it out!' I hissed.

'Sure. Going home is cool. But Robbie, I want you to know – well, thanks. If it hadn't been for you things would have been dead boring these last few weeks.'

'Oh, that's okay...'

'By the way, Robbie, have you seen your friend J today? There was a man here asking for him. I mean, he was in the road, sort of looking around. I wondered if he might be a sort of relation of his. Remember when you said he had no family.'

'Yeah? He told me he was an orphan. What was this man like?'

'Oh just sort of ordinary, you know. Sounded sort of foreign.'

'I'll go and see him when I get back.' Then there was a long pause. Awkward. 'Well, anyway, Tara, good luck!'

'Oh, here's Oliver...'

'Don't forget to write!'

'I will.'

'Well, bye.'

'You've been sweet.'

'Bye!'

I put the phone down with mixed feelings. I didn't like leavings, saying goodbyes. Alan was taking the mickey, going 'Don't forget to write!' and trying to kiss me. I had to chase him halfway down the street before I could land a good kick on him.

* * *

Later, it came out that Jorgenssen's actions had been aided by an unlucky twist of fate. He had entered Dounby and driven slowly down to the harbour and parked at the end of the pier. He had walked past Sandy Stokes sitting outside his café with a knotted handkerchief on his head, looking like a character from Monty Python's Flying Circus. Sandy Stokes had known right away of course that Jorgenssen was a villain – he said – although he had been strangely reluctant to come forward as a witness. Jorgenssen had been seen by lots of people. He stuck out like a sore thumb. He had been seen ascending the Braeheid and it was obvious he was looking for something. There are almost no street signs in Dounby. He had been seen climbing the hill, all the way to the top; methodically investigating the side streets and alleys – and at the top, where the road levels out, he had been seen turning to look back. Then he was observed speaking to a young woman in a garden, a girl with short white-blonde hair. This was Tara of course, and she gave him directions. He set off back down the hill, seemed to find the street he was looking for but there was no sign of a motorbike. He was seen standing there rubbing the back of his neck, and then walking slowly back to his car.

Several people saw Jorgenssen standing beside his car watching the woman intently. Her long dark hair gave her the look of a film actress he said at the trial whom he had remembered from his childhood cinema-visits in Bergen. He was seen leaning over the bonnet of his car, toying with the keys as if deciding what to do. He got into the car, sat for a moment, then climbed out again and went over to sit on the low wall. Those who were watching him – and in Dounby everyone watches strangers – said that he was leering at her. He spoke to her and she replied. Nobody was near enough to hear what was said but Xanthe later told the court that what he had said to her was: 'You know guy – he has motorbike? Young guy, he living here, yes?'

What Xanthe had said to him was: 'I do know a young man who has a motorbike.'

And Jorgenssen had then said: 'Lady. Him I know too. Motorbiker. For him I look. Not at home, no.'

'He is a friend of mine... Mr...?'

'Ah. Jorgenssen. Jorg-en-ssen. You know where he is?'

Xanthe claimed that she had merely pointed vaguely westwards and said: 'Perhaps you might find him at the beach.' Her face, according to the court reporter was 'drawn and pale' as she gave this testimony and her voice was so low that the High Court Judge several times had to ask her to speak louder.

But Jorgenssen was confused. He could see that the shingle beach was empty. He got back in his car and drove up to the main road. He had apparently intended returning to Duncairn but at the junction noticed the sign for Redstanes Caravan Park & Beach so he took a right turn. Further on, he saw the sign for Dounby Head and it occurred to him that he might see any local beaches by going out onto the headland, so he took the first right and was heading out to the auto Light when by pure chance or bad luck he spotted the motorbike parked off the road at the top of the cliff.

It was a long time before the final part of the tragedy was sketched. Big J had realised that the man was watching him. He stood up and sauntered over the sand to speak to the stranger who sat on the rock moodily glaring down the beach at the starkness of the shadow cast by the Anvil Stane.

'Nice day, eh? Are you looking for someone?' J would probably have inquired. You can imagine him smiling, scuffing his bare feet in the sand.

There would have been something remarkably still about the stranger, restrained and self-contained. And he must have looked so odd, outlined against the sea, solemn, out of place on a sunny beach. Jorgenssen would have asked about the motorbike and Big J would have happily admitted to owning it. The name of Tish might have puzzled J. He would still be smiling, puzzled but fearless – he had nothing to fear. J would have acknowledged the name though and maybe Jorgenssen noticed that. What happened next was all in Jorgenssen's plan. He was justified. He was certain. There was nothing J could do. Maybe J would have tried to tell him about Oliver Harwood. It wouldn't have mattered anyway.

The derrickman would have whipped the wrench out of his inner pocket. Swung it in a powerful arc. Big J probably never even saw it. The doctors were to count at least eight distinct blows to the cranium, more to the torso.

Jorgenssen had left him there, bleeding, unconscious, as the tide collected and forced itself between the Witches' Craig and the Anvil Stane. The tide would have made a waterstorm around his head, a whirling world of lost sensations and the stolen breath of everything living. The police estimated that it was four hours before anyone noticed the motorbike standing guard on the cliff and chanced to glance over at the beach. One hour later and it would have been too dark to see Big J drifting in the surf.

But Big J did not die. He had fallen on his back – which
turned out to be very lucky – for hardly any water had got
into his lungs. He had serious head injuries and broken
ribs, punctured lung, ruptured spleen, broken nose. He
was barely recognisable on the trolley that wheeled him
out from several emergency operations at Duncairn
Infirmary, according to reports. There were medical
complications and the expert opinion was that he had
been lucky to survive. At first, I phoned a few times, but
he was too badly injured to speak and when I finally
visited him on the ward, he was asleep, heavily sedated. I
couldn't talk to him. I stood there, feeling miserable,
looking at his almost unrecognisable face beneath the
bandages. Then I got the bus back to Dounby and, to an
extent, forgot him. We all did. I sold his bike and kept
the money for him. It was many weeks before he returned
to Dounby and by that time Xanthe had gone, and Oliver,
and the house was up for sale. The police arrested
Jorgenssen. He was brought to trial and convicted of
grievous bodily harm although found not guilty on the
attempted murder charge. He accepted the verdict with
stoic fortitude – or so I imagined as I watched him on TV
being led out in handcuffs to a police van – and whether
he understood his error or cared, I couldn't say. I

remember reading a small article about the verdict in a national newspaper. The procurator fiscal described his actions as those of an irresponsible vigilante. Whether Oliver was responsible for the injuries to Tish I can only speculate and whether the police interviewed him or not is something about which I have no knowledge.

What I do know is that somebody climbed down to our beach one day and destroyed Big J's shelter and took away the tarpaulin. They stole his radio and smashed everything else. Ed and I were horrified when we found it.

'He's lying in hospital!' I raged. 'Who do you think did it?'

'Who knows. Some jealous bugger.'

'Well, there were a lot of those.'

A few days later, I walked on the beach with Xanthe. (I still think of her as Mrs Pritchard of course.) It was the second last time I ever spoke to her. We were very gloomy as she drove us there in the car. Parked and then we picked our way down. We walked to where Big J's shelter had stood and tried to find something valuable to hold on to, some evidence about it all.

'He's ruined the place for me now,' she said, hands on hips looking at the horizon. 'With his acquisitiveness. His determination to be the only possessor. He couldn't just enjoy...' she frowned at the sand... 'what is to be enjoyed and understand that it's not all up for grabs. Oh, Roberto, how sad I am that I can't come back next summer. He's ruined that for me. Serge will be pleased,' she ended acidly.

'I don't see why you can't.'

'For a start, Oliver is selling the place.'

'But there are other bungalows you could rent?'

She smiled benignly at me. 'Ah, Robbie, why couldn't he be more like you?' She put her arm in mine and we walked along the sand. 'Why couldn't he understand that just because there's a beach, sunshine and two people of the opposite sex walking along in the sand, that doesn't mean it's the perfect romance. For ever and ever and ever.'

'So it's all over?'

'Now, you – you've never been anything but pleasant and friendly without all this... complication, this possession thing. I don't know. I really don't.'

I looked at his slashed mattress and the broken things that marked his beach refuge, now scattered and abused. What did Big J truly possess? Almost nothing. Very little of the world's things, even those items like parents and family which others take for granted. Was it surprising that he had tried to possess the one thing that had attracted him – which seemed capable of taking him away from nowhere – to somewhere? All he had was his greatness, his heroism and his legend, in the minds of the few who knew of it. Even if that was to prove a chimera in my own imagination and no one else's. Of course, it wasn't till much later that I understood that when you separated layer from layer of his charm... his poise... to get to the bottom of what made him The Big J – you found there was nothing exceptional there. It took me a long time to discover that – long after I'd left Dounby – but it didn't tarnish my perception of him at all.

'But what went wrong?' I pleaded. 'You seemed so right together.'

'Oh, we were. That's just it.'

I was never to get a better explanation and to a great extent what happened between them remained a mystery. Not the obvious of course. I knew how that worked – but how such intensity, joy, passion, whatever... could just turn upon itself and dissolve to nothing. That was new to me. The sourness of it all. But what I also knew was how he had impacted upon her, though she might not fully admit it. I had seen how she was with him at the party on the beach. I had seen how girlish she had become around him. He had transformed her into a love-struck teenager in some clumsy but inexorable way. She couldn't deny it. Not that I ever asked her to. And at the back of my mind something kept nagging me and nagging me but I was never able to put my finger on what it was. Before she left, in our final conversation, she told me Tara had gone back to stay with her mother in London. Later, I heard she had got into fashion school and no doubt enjoys her time there among the other wealthy, egotistical and socially irrelevant giraffes.

I never spoke to Big J again. And I never did give him the money for the bike. By the time he came out of hospital, I was in Glasgow, looking for digs, preparing myself for Uni. Other worlds to explore. It was a year before I visited and he wasn't around then. My mother and stepfather moved to Hull and still live there. I visited once. Now I just phone every now and again. If you've been to Hull you'll know what I mean.

Nikki and Loren returned to Dounby the next summer, married local guys and settled in Gardyne. They live practically next door to each other. They've gained a lot of weight. Loren works as a barmaid in the Fisherman's Arms and Nikki, who is divorced, is a full-time mother. Of the others, Rachel Fyves lives in Duncairn, she's lost her looks and her hair is blonde these days. Alan's a boffin of course, sometimes I see him on the telly. Yvie and Lila have disappeared but just last year, I read in the paper that our giraffe had got engaged to an English actor with famously floppy hair – and a week later, more headlines – it was all off. Lucky escape, there, Robbie!

Heather Lowdy astounded us all though. She travelled the world with a succession of boyfriends, got a better degree than me, settled for a while in Abu Dhabi and married a Sheikh. She has two children and is the author of a bestselling guidebook. She visits her parents every Christmas in a big entourage that draw everybody out to doors to watch. Abdul is the only Sheikh to set foot in Dounby. Every two years her picture appears on the jacket of a new book and I have made space on my shelf for more. She'll be twenty-five this year.

* * *

Yesterday, on my day off, I drove up the motorway and into quieter roads and then by the back roads through the little villages. It was like taking a history lesson of my own backyard. Auchtergat, Auldloof, Braes O' Dour and the kirkyard at Montquhitter. I read again the cursory inscription on my father's stone and on those of my great-uncles. A drizzle seeming to emanate from the surrounding gentle hills suited my mood. Then I took the undulating, swooping road to the coast but my memory was already threadbare and I found myself lost somewhere near Redstanes. I took an unfamiliar main road back to the Dounby junction and recalled the mellow timbre of Xanthe Pritchard-Benz cooing 'My dear Roberto...' her hand on my knee – and then slowly came out to the village, swallowing unfamiliar air. It seemed long ago, in my parents' lifetimes, or my grandparents' and yet it was like yesterday. Breeks was already dead, victim of the terrible carnage on Piper Alpha.

And as I stood leaning on the dyke at the car park looking down, listening to those gulls, I caught sight of Big J at the corner of Main Street and Strait Path, just below the telephone box, on the concrete steps. I couldn't believe what I was seeing. He was halfway up and he was halfway down, standing holding the rail, looking away out to sea. He had gained a lot of weight and his hair, even at that distance, was streaked with grey. I noted the wheeled bin at the top of the steps and his council donkey jacket, the red rubber gloves, and I did not go down. I felt my heart pounding and pounding. I wanted to go down and talk to him but I stood watching, waiting, hoping for him to make a move, to go up or to go back down, to get on with his business, but he did not. What he was seeing on the horizon was of much more interest to him than what was around him. He just stood and stood. After a few minutes, I turned away and got back in the car, my eyes wet with painful memories of things beyond my control, which will stay with me forever and ever and ever.